Dawn and the Big Sleepover

Other books by
Ann M. Martin

Ma and Pa Dracula
Yours Turly, Shirley
Ten Kids, No Pets
Slam Book
Just a Summer Romance
Missing Since Monday
With You and Without You
Me and Katie (the Pest)
Stage Fright
Inside Out
Bummer Summer

BABY-SITTERS LITTLE SISTER series
THE BABY-SITTERS CLUB series
(see back of the book for a complete listing)

Dawn and the Big Sleepover

Ann M. Martin

SCHOLASTIC INC.
New York Toronto London Auckland Sydney

Special thanks to
Harry and Sandy Colt
for their information
on Zuni
culture.

Cover art by Hodges Soileau

ISBN 0-590-43573-6

12 11 10 9 8 7 6 5 4 3 1 2 3 4 5 6/9

Printed in the U.S.A. 40

First Scholastic printing, May 1991

The author gratefully acknowledges
Peter Lerangis
for his help in
preparing this manuscript.

Dawn and the Big Sleepover

"Can I read Rachel's letter first? Can I?"

Vanessa Pike was jumping up and down with excitement. She swung a letter and photo in the air, practically hitting me in the face.

"Me next!" Jordan Pike said.

"Me next!" Margo Pike said.

"Me next!" Adam Pike said.

"Come on, guys, sit down," Mallory Pike said.

Have you ever baby-sat for a family of eight kids? Well, welcome to the Pikes' house. Fortunately, sitting for them usually involves *two* of us members of the Baby-sitters Club. Unfortunately, eight kids is a lot, even for us.

Actually, they're really good kids — most of the time. One of them, Mallory, is a member of our club (more about the BSC later). Mal is eleven and a *great* sitter. She and I were both looking after her brothers and sisters that night.

Who am I? I'm Dawn Schafer. I'm thirteen, and I've lived in Stoneybrook, Connecticut, since seventh grade. I used to live in California, and if you met me, you *might* say, "It figures." I have *long* blonde hair and blue eyes, and I'm into health foods and sunshine (not that *every* California girl is like that, but that's what a lot of people think). Anyway, I moved here with my mom and my younger brother, Jeff, after my parents divorced. Stoneybrook was the town my mother grew up in, and *her* parents still live here. I liked it right away, but Jeff hated it and ended up moving back to California to live with our dad. (He seems happy now, but Mom and I miss him a lot.) We live in a fantastic old farmhouse that was built in 1795. It has a barn with a secret passage that leads right to my bedroom! Since my mom remarried, my stepfather and stepsister live with us (more on them later, too).

So that's me. Now back to the Pikes' house. Our heroes were on the horns of a dilemma (they weren't really, but I read that once in a book, and it cracked me up). Adam, Jordan, and Byron (ten-year-old triplets); Vanessa (who's nine); Nicky (eight); and Margo (seven) were incredibly excited about the letters and photos they had gotten from their pen pals. Anyway, if you've been keeping count, you've noticed I left out one Pike. That's Claire, who's five. She's only in kindergarten, so she wasn't involved in Pens Across America.

I guess I should explain that Pens Across America is a national pen pal program for second- through fifth-graders. The schools that take part are called "sister schools." (Why? I don't know. *All* the kids participate, not just girls. It should be "sibling schools" or something.) For a few weeks, the kids at Stoneybrook Elementary School (SES) had been writing to . . . Zunis! "Zuni" is the name of a Native American tribe in New Mexico, and they have an elementary school on their reservation. (Their reservation is also called Zuni.)

None of the kids had ever met their pen pals, but it was amazing how close they felt. Take Vanessa. She was *dying* to read the letter from her pen pal, Rachel. You'd think Rachel was a long-lost sister or something (as if Vanessa didn't have enough sisters).

"Let's see her picture first!" Margo said.

All of us leaned over the coffee table to look at the photograph.

"She's pretty," Margo said. "I wish *my* pen pal was smiling." She held out a photo of a girl with a grim expression.

Vanessa shrugged. "Maybe she has braces."

"Yuk," was Adam's remark.

"Let's see *your* pen pal, Adam," Margo added. "I bet he's a dork."

"He is not," Adam replied. "He looks just like the kids in your pictures."

Margo giggled. "He looks like a *girl?*"

"No!" Adam said gloomily. "I mean, he just looks . . . you know, like a kid." He dug a folded-up envelope out of his pocket, then took out a crumpled school photo of a smiling boy with short black hair. Across the bottom in pen it said, YOUR FRIEND, CONRAD.

"What did you expect him to look like?" Vanessa asked.

"I don't know . . ." Adam said. "Like an Indian, I guess."

"He wants to see headdresses and costumes," Byron said. "Like on TV."

"And warpaint! *Woo-woo-woo-woo!*" Jordan whooped.

"*No* . . ." Adam said, turning red.

"Guys, come on!" Mal called out.

I think Adam *did* want to see headdresses and tepees and stuff — and he was feeling guilty about it. Mal had lectured him about stereotyping, and all the kids in his school had learned about how the modern Zunis really live.

"He's a *Native American,* Adam," Mallory said, as if she'd said it a hundred times before, which was probably true. "*Indians* are from India. You should know that by now, especially after three letters."

"I know," Adam said with a sigh. "But Indians — uh, Native Americans — are supposed to have names like, you know, Chief Rocking Horse and Joe Crescent Moon . . ." Adam looked forlornly at his letter. "Not Conrad White."

"Maybe it's short for White Horse," Nicky suggested.

"Or White Smoke Signals," Margo piped up.

I decided to interrupt this conversation. "Adam, a *lot* of the pen pals have English-sounding names. It doesn't mean they're not Native Americans."

"My pen pal's named Wendy Jackson," Margo reminded him.

Nicky nodded. "Mine's Joey Evans."

Suddenly, Vanessa exclaimed, "I thought I was going to *read!*"

"You are!" I said. "Okay, guys, listen up. Presenting . . ." (I gave a little dramatic gesture with my arms) "Vanessa!"

Vanessa held up her letter and started to read. This is how it went:

" 'Dear Vanessa,

" 'Hi. I really liked your letter. I mostly liked hearing about your family. It must be fun to have triplets in the house.' " Vanessa stopped reading and said under her breath, "That's what she thinks."

"Hey!" Jordan blurted out.

She quickly went on, " 'My family has twelve people. I'm the youngest. There are my brothers John and James; my sister, April; my parents; three grandparents (the fourth one is dead); my aunts Martha and Connie; and my uncle Bob. My brother John is in California now. He's nineteen, and he's allowed to fight forest fires. My dad says he can make a lot of money doing that. I miss him. I have a question for you. Why don't your relatives live with you? It must be hard to get all the work done.' "

"They *all* live in the same *house?*" Nicky said. "It must be super huge."

"If you'd *listen*, you'd find out," Vanessa answered. She cleared her throat and continued:

" 'Our teacher, Mrs. Randall, is really nice. She's an Anglo, like you. She said we should tell you about the way Zunis live — about our houses and our parents' jobs and our customs and stuff. Well, we live in a pueblo. That's like a village, with lots of houses around a plaza. Our houses are called adobe houses, and they're made of clay and wood. They have flat roofs, and they're one story high. Maybe that sounds strange to you, but it's not. We have electricity and running water and TVs and stuff like that. We speak Zuni at home with our families. Most of the moms and dads make great jewelry to sell at the stores in town. I asked my mom if I could send you a bracelet but she said maybe next time.

" 'Yours truly, Rachel Redriver.' "

Everyone began talking at once:

"See? *She* has an Indian name!" Adam said.

"What's an Anglo?" Claire piped up.

"A white person, I think," Mal answered.

"I'm next!" Jordan called out. He unwrinkled his letter and began to read, stumbling over the big words:

" 'Dear Jordan,

" 'Mrs. Randall is making me tell you about Sha'la'ko. [Jordan had a *real* rough time with that one.] It's a big festival that we Zunis have for the new year. Our new year starts in December. Every year there are eight special Sha'la'ko houses. This year ours is one! My mom has been fixing the house for months. When the sun goes down on the first day of Sha'la'ko, dancers come into all the rooms to bless the house. They dance all night without stopping. They wear masks and feathers and stuff, and we're supposed to throw cornmeal at them for good luck. All the kids are allowed to stay up to watch.

" 'Do you have the Teenage Mutant Ninja Turtles movie there? It's great! What about Nintendo? Let me know which video games you like!' "

Suddenly Jordan started to laugh, then instantly stopped.

"What?" Vanessa asked.

"Nothing," Jordan said, hiding his letter. "That's all he wrote."

"No, there's more," Vanessa insisted, grabbing Jordan's letter. "Come on, let's *see* it!"

"Hey!" Jordan yelled. *"Dawn!* She's — "

Before I could do anything, Vanessa started reading in a singsong voice. " 'P.S. Y-may eacher-tay ells-smay ike-lay a-hay ow-cay . . .' " She paused for a moment, then her eyes lit up. "Oooh . . ."

"My teacher smells like a cow!" Adam cried out. "That's pig Latin!"

"Ew! Ew!" Margo said.

Well, you'd think it was the most clever thing anyone had ever thought of. All the other kids exploded with giggles — even Claire, who had been pretty quiet since she didn't have a pen pal herself. "Adam, silly-billy-goo-goo," she squealed.

"Did you teach Sam that, Jordan?" Adam demanded. (Sam is Adam's pen pal.)

Byron looked disappointed. "I thought that was our secret language."

"It's okay, Byron," Jordan said. "Sam's a good guy, and I made him promise not to tell anyone."

Byron nodded seriously (he's the most sensitive of the triplets), and I kept myself from laughing. As if their secret would really be *ruined* because some kids clear across the country found out.

"Look, you guys," Mal continued, "your pen pals all sent you pictures. Why don't you think about what you can send *them?*"

That idea must have gone over well, because the kids all fell silent. I wouldn't have thought of that, but leave it to Mal. Really, she's a perfect big sister. As you can see, she is very practical and smart and cool under pressure. Not to mention creative. Her goal in life is to write and illustrate children's books, and I know she'll be great at it. (The problem is, Mal's convinced her parents will never let her grow up. They still won't let her wear wild clothes or get contacts.)

Anyway, Mal's idea was really catching fire. Even Adam was getting into it. He ran into his room and emerged seconds later with a big, felt Stoneybrook pennant. "This is what I'm going to send!"

"Me too!" Byron shouted.

"Me three!" Jordan pitched in, smiling at his own joke.

"Wait!" I said. "You can't all send the same thing."

"Yeah, that's boring," Vanessa said.

Margo jumped up. "How about Stoneybrook decals?"

"Or bumper stickers!" Byron added.

Mal nodded. "Stoneybrook souvenirs would be great — but they're not as special as the pictures they sent you."

"We don't *have* our school photos yet," Nicky said with a shrug.

I put my two cents in. "What kinds of things do we have in Connecticut that they might not have out there?"

"Cable TV?" Adam suggested.

"Rain," Nicky said. "Ms. Farnsworth told us the weather is always sunny out there."

Vanessa groaned. "Really great ideas, guys. Did you forget to put in your brains this morning?"

"Whatever you say bounces off me and sticks to you," Adam said.

"We could get something from the mall!" Jordan blurted out. "Like T-shirts with our pictures on them."

"Or some stationery!" Vanessa said.

Anyway, that's pretty much how it went that afternoon at the Pikes'. That was back when the pen pal program was fun. Back when us older kids weren't involved. Simple. Easy.

If only I had known what was about to happen.

By the time Mrs. Pike got home from her trustees meeting at the Stoneybrook Public Library, the kids were hard at work writing letters. Adam had decided he'd send the pennant, and Nicky would send the decals. Byron was going to ask his dad if he could take some pictures of the family, Vanessa planned to write a poem, and Jordan wanted to tape-record himself playing the piano. Margo was still thinking.

As I walked home, all I could think about were the Zunis. They sounded fascinating. I was dying to know more about their lifestyle, and Sha'la'ko, and a million other things. In a way, I felt kind of sad. I wished it were *our* school that was in the Pens Across America program.

"Hi, Mary Anne," I said to my stepsister, who was in the living room.

Mary Anne took one look at my face and

said, "Don't tell me. The triplets flooded the sink."

"No," I said.

"Nicky broke Vanessa's glasses."

"No!"

"Margo got sick."

I smiled. "Mary Anne, do I look *that* tired?"

Before Mary Anne could answer, my mom called out from the kitchen, "Hi, sweetheart!"

One thing I should say about my mom. She's *not* Julia Child. I mean, she can throw together a decent salad, but anything else is "eat at your own risk." The same thing with housework. She sort of loses interest halfway through. And Richard, my stepfather, is exactly the opposite — super organized. I was happy to see him in the kitchen, seasoning some sort of delicious-smelling casserole.

"Hi!" I called back, plopping onto the living room couch. "I'll come in and help in a minute."

"That's okay, honey," my mom said. "Everything's almost ready."

"You and Mary Anne can set the table in about ten minutes," Richard said.

"Sure," I replied.

Mary Anne was still looking at me with that "I know something's wrong" expression on her face.

"The kids were rowdy, but not too bad," I said. "They were working on their pen pal letters."

Mary Anne nodded. "That project sounds like a lot of fun."

"Yeah," I answered. "The kids love it. And to tell you the truth, I'm really disappointed that *we* can't be in the program, just because we're older."

"It's sort of like what my dad says sometimes: 'Youth is wasted on the young.' " Mary Anne smiled. "Maybe you can write the Zuni elementary school and ask about finding a pen pal of your own in their middle school."

That wasn't a bad idea. See what a great stepsister I have? Sometimes I think Mary Anne can read my mind.

Okay. I promised I'd tell you about my stepfamily, so here goes. Mary Anne Spier is my best friend in the world. As you can see, she's a good listener, sensitive and patient. Mary Anne's also very shy and she cries easily. She was one of the first people I met when I moved to Connecticut — *before* she was my stepsister, of course. Back then she wore her hair in pigtails and dressed in little-girl clothes, and had to be home by nine o'clock (in *seventh grade*). That's because her dad (Richard) set the rules. See, Mary Anne's mom died when Mary Anne was little, then *Richard's* parents died — so Mary Anne was all he had left, and he became *very* protective of her.

Anyway, guess who my mom used to date when she was at Stoneybrook High. *Richard.* When Mary Anne and I found this out, we got them back together and — *ta-da!* — they got married. Richard has loosened up a lot, and Mary Anne is no longer the oldest baby in Stoneybrook. As a matter of fact, she's the only one of us BSC members who has ever had a steady boyfriend. His name was (*is* — Mary Anne broke up with him but he's still alive) Logan Bruno. Mary Anne, by the way, is our club's secretary.

You probably want to know about the other club members. Here goes. First of all, they're the greatest friends I could imagine having. If you've ever moved to a school in the middle of the year, you know how hard it is to meet people. Well, the BSC made me feel totally welcome. Everyone was open and friendly, which was great, because nothing turns me off more than cliques where everyone dresses and sounds alike. Not that there are *never* any conflicts in the BSC, but everyone respects everyone else's personality.

And there are *lots* of different personalities.

Kristy Thomas, for example. She's the president of the BSC, and the one who thought up the whole thing. As you can guess, she really knows how to get things done — and she *knows* she knows. What I mean is, she can be a little loud and bossy. (A little? A *lot* sometimes.) She's always full of ideas and can be counted on to be mature and levelheaded in any emergency. Which you might not guess if you saw her. She seems younger than thirteen, probably because she's the shortest one in the class and she doesn't seem to care about boys. Also, she *never* worries about the way she looks. A turtleneck shirt, jeans, running shoes, no makeup — that's Kristy. Her two big interests are children (the main requirement for being in the BSC) and sports. She's even figured out a way to combine the two, by organizing a softball team for kids who don't play in Little League. (A true Kristy idea.)

What a family life *she* has. It makes mine look simple. Really, it's sort of like a fairy tale . . . The Saga of Kristy, Chapter 1: Kristy's dad walks out on the family — just heads out the door and never looks back. He leaves his wife with a newborn baby (David Michael), Kristy, and two older brothers (Sam and Charlie). Chapter 2: Mrs. Thomas finds a job and raises all four kids *herself*. Chapter 3: Six years later, Sam and Charlie are in high school, Kristy is president of the most brilliant baby-sitting organization in history, and David Michael is six. Along comes Watson Brewer, a divorced millionaire. He sweeps Mrs. Thomas off her feet (which is hard to imagine — he's balding and quiet and likes gardening), and they fall in love. Kristy hates the idea of having a stepfamily, but . . . Chapter 4: She finally comes around and Watson marries her mother. The Thomas family moves across town to Watson's mansion, where everyone has their own room — even Watson's kids, Karen and Andrew, who only live there every other weekend and for two weeks in the summer. Everyone lives happily ever after. Epilogue: The Thomas/Brewer family decides to adopt a two-year-old Vietnamese girl, whom they call Emily Michelle. Now the mansion is beginning to look like a small town, so Nannie (Kristy's grandmother) moves in to help take care of the kids. And the saga continues.

You may find it hard to believe, but loud Kristy and shy Mary Anne have been best friends practically since birth. (That's what I mean about the BSC — everyone fits together.)

Now. On to Claudia. Claudia Kishi, that is. She's our vice-president. She's Japanese-American and totally stunning, with silky black hair, almond-shaped eyes, and a perfect complexion. She's got a great figure, too, despite the fact that she is a junk food *fanatic*. You can't spend two minutes in Claudia's room without her pulling a Ring-Ding or a Twinkie or a Snickers bar out of some hiding place. She's got all kinds of art supplies, too, but those are out in the open. Claudia's main thing (besides junk food) is *art*. You name it, she can do it well — painting, drawing, sculpting, jewelry making . . . even the way she *dresses* is artistic. For instance, she walked into school today wearing a bright yellow, oversize man's jacket with rolled-up sleeves; a wide paisley tie right out of the nineteen-sixties; orange stirrup pants; ankle boots; and huge hoop earrings — and you know what? On her, it looked totally cool.

Oh, another passion of Claud's is Nancy Drew books. She has *them* hidden around her room, too, because her parents don't approve of them. They think she should be reading classics or textbooks, like her sister, Janine. Janine's a certified genius, with one of the highest IQs anyone's ever heard of. (She's the kind of person who finds mistakes in the *dictionary*.) She and Claudia get along okay, but they couldn't be more different. Claudia doesn't do very well in school — probably because she always feels she can't compete with Janine. Which is too bad, because Claudia's really smart. Oh, well, she'll become a famous artist someday and then it won't matter what grades she got in school.

Claudia's best friend is Stacey McGill, who is our treasurer. Stacey is as sophisticated as Claud, and she also has a flair for wild clothes and jewelry. They both have boyfriends sometimes, although no one steady. But that's where the similarities end. For one thing, Stacey's got blonde hair and blue eyes, she's an only child, and — here's the best part — she's from New York City! Just like I'm a California girl at heart, Stacey's a real New Yorker. She has a map of the city on her wall, and something called an alternate-side-of-the-street-parking calendar, with cartoons about car-parking (they're really dumb, but New Yorkers supposedly find them hilarious). Stacey moved to Stoneybrook when her dad was transferred here (he's a businessman) — then, when he was transferred *again*, she moved back to New York. But less than a year after they settled into a new apartment, her parents told her they were getting a divorce — and Stacey moved with her mother *back* to Stoneybrook. She could have chosen to stay in the city, but she didn't. That was a tough decision for her, but we were thrilled when she came back.

Stacey's life is complicated by one other thing, if you can believe it. She has diabetes.

That's a disease in which your body has trouble controlling the level of sugar in your blood. Stacey has to be on a strict diet for life (meaning no sweets) — and she has to give herself daily injections of a drug called insulin. To tell you the truth, I still don't know how she can watch Claudia pull out candy left and right and not go totally crazy.

There are two junior officers in the BSC — "junior" because they're in sixth grade (the rest of us are in eighth grade). You know one of them already — Mal. The other one is Jessica (Jessi) Ramsey. She and Mal are best friends. Both of them love to read and are crazy about horses. Jessi's the oldest in her family, just like Mal, but she has only one sister (Becca, short for Rebecca) and one brother (Squirt, short for Squirt). Actually, Squirt's real name is John Philip Ramsey, Jr., but he was really tiny when he was born, and some nurses at the hospital gave him the nickname. Becca is eight and a half and Squirt is a little over a year.

Jessi's big talent is ballet dancing and she wants to be a pro. I have to say, she *is* good, and she doesn't even get stage fright. Jessi is also the BSC's only black member. The Ramseys are one of the only black families in Stoneybrook, by the way. Some of the people here gave Jessi's family a rough time at first, but fortunately things have calmed down and the Ramseys are much happier.

Well, those are the club members. I'll tell you about the club itself in a little while, so stick around!

Back in our house, Richard was putting trivets on the table. Even Mom was hard at work, setting place mats and filling a water pitcher.

Suddenly I was famished — and feeling a lot more energetic than I had when I got back from the Pikes'.

That Friday Mary Anne and I rode our bikes to our club meeting as usual. Where were we heading? Claudia's house. Her bedroom is the official meeting place of the Baby-sitters Club for one very important reason — she's the only one of us who has her own private telephone. (That's also the main reason Claudia is the club vice-president.)

It was three days after my job at the Pikes', and to tell you the truth, I had sort of forgotten about Pens Across America and the Zunis. All I was thinking about was the same thing I think about whenever I go to a BSC meeting on Friday: *no school tomorrow*. We also meet on Mondays and Wednesdays (5:30 to 6:00 is our meeting time on all days), but Friday meetings are my favorites. Everyone is so relaxed.

Usually.

I'm dying to tell you what happened at this meeting, but first let me explain a few things about the club. Actually, *club* is sort of the wrong word for it, because it's really a business (but I guess "Baby-sitters Company" would sound kind of strange). When Kristy thought up the idea for the club we were all in seventh grade. Back then, B.W. (Before Watson), Kristy and her two older brothers used to take turns baby-sitting for David Michael. One day, when none of them could sit, Mrs. Thomas called to try to find an outside sitter . . . and called . . . and called, but no one was free. She was on the horns of a dilemma (sorry). Well, that's when something clicked inside Kristy's mind. Wouldn't it be great if a parent could dial one number and reach a whole bunch of baby-sitters!

The Baby-sitters Club was born. Right away, Kristy got Mary Anne, Claudia, and then Stacey to become the first members. They decided on the meeting times, when people could call and line up a sitter. Then the four of them could fill the jobs, and everyone would be happy. To get customers, they put an ad in the Stoneybrook paper and distributed fliers throughout their neighborhoods. Well, the rest is history. Kristy's great idea caught on like crazy. When I moved to Stoneybrook that January, they had so much business they couldn't *wait* to take in a new member (lucky me). Before long, there were two associate members — Logan Bruno and a friend of Kristy's named Shannon Kilbourne. (They're strictly backup people we call on if we're all busy.) Jessi and Mallory became our junior officers when Stacey moved to New York — and they stayed in the club even when Stacey moved back (once a club member, always a club member).

Kristy, as I said, is the club president. She runs the meetings and constantly comes up with new plans and ideas — like a summer play group; a special Mothers' Day event, when we took the kids to a carnival as a gift to our clients; and, of course, Kid-Kits. They're boxes filled with our old games, books, toys, coloring books, paper, and crayons. Each of us has one, and we take them on our jobs sometimes. Let me tell you, kids *love* them.

Kristy also thought up the idea of the club notebook. That's our official diary. We have to write about every single job we take — *and* read all the other entries. It's how we keep track of our kids' likes, dislikes, new habits, things like that. It's also a record of how each of us has dealt with baby-sitting problems. Writing in it is not my favorite thing to do, but I realize it helps keep us prepared.

I mentioned already that Claudia is our VP. To be honest, she doesn't do a whole lot at the meetings, but it *is* her phone, and we *do* eat all her junk food, so it is only right that she should be an officer.

Mary Anne is our secretary. She's in charge of the club record book (not to be confused with the *note*book I just mentioned). The record book is a list of clients' names, addresses, and phone numbers, a record of how much money we make, *and* our weekly sitting schedule. You can imagine what it's like to keep track of that for seven girls, what with Claud's art classes, Jessi's dance lessons, and Mal's orthodontist appointments (just to name a few problems). I'll tell you, it makes me dizzy just to *look* at the book, but you know what? Mary Anne has never — I mean *never* — made a mistake. She keeps track of it all in her tidy handwriting.

As treasurer, Stacey handles the money. She's one of these people who can add and subtract numbers in her head like a calculator, so she's perfect for the job. At every Monday meeting, she collects club dues from us. Yes, dues. We all grumble about it, but we understand how necessary it is. The money goes to group expenses, like helping out with Claud's phone bill, paying Charlie for driving Kristy to and from meetings (Watson's mansion is pretty far away), buying new things for the Kid-Kits, and (if there's any left over) a club pizza party or sleepover now and then. Stacey is *very* thrifty. She keeps track of every penny and hates to spend it unless it's absolutely necessary.

I like being the alternate officer. I'm sort of an understudy. If someone can't make a meeting, I get to take over her job. For a while, when Stacey moved to New York, I was the club treasurer. But I'm not a math genius, so I was happy to return the job to her when she moved back. So far I've filled in for just about everyone.

Our two junior officers, Mal and Jessi, aren't allowed to take late sitting jobs unless they're at their own homes. So they do a lot of the daytime sitting, and that frees the rest of us up at night.

Okay, now you know all there is to know about the club. Finally I can tell you about our meeting.

Mary Anne and I arrived early that day. Claudia greeted us at the door to her room with her hair in a ponytail on top of her head, held up by a huge barrette in the shape of a bone, like Pebbles in *The Flintstones*. It made her hair bounce when she moved. She was even wearing a Pebbles-type outfit — a pink, off-the-shoulder blouse with huge polka dots and a ragged bottom over black tights. On anyone else it would have looked dumb or babyish, but on Claudia it looked cool.

As we walked into her room, her clock read 5:23. There were a few schoolbooks on her bed — all closed — and a huge pad of paper where she had been sketching some abstract drawings of a half-human, half-horse (at least that's what it looked like).

"Have you tried these, Mary Anne?" Claud said, reaching under her pillow to pull out some new kind of dark-chocolate caramel.

"Nope," Mary Anne said.

"Have one," Claud offered. Then she lay flat on her stomach and pulled a big bag of pretzels from under her bed. "These are for you, Dawn."

She didn't have to twist our arms. We each got into position on Claud's bed — sitting cross-legged, leaning slightly forward, and chewing. That's how we sit in most of the meetings. (Stacey and I switch off sometimes — one of us sits in Claudia's desk chair, with the chair backward and our chin resting on the top rung.)

"Any calls?" I asked. Sometimes clients forget when our meetings are and call us at odd hours.

"Nnrrrp," Claudia said with her mouth full.

We immediately started giggling, and I could feel a lump of pretzel starting to go up my nose, which made me giggle even more. That made Mary Anne giggle more. Claudia put her hand over her mouth and made some strange snorting noise that she obviously couldn't help.

Wouldn't you know it was at that moment that Kristy walked in. "What happened?" she said innocently.

Well, you know about giggling. Once you start, everything seems funny. We were rolling on the bed now, and Kristy looked like she was ready to commit us. She shook her head and climbed into Claud's director's chair.

Before long, Stacey arrived, then Jessi. By that time, we were pretty much under control, chatting and munching. Stacey sat in the desk chair, exactly the way I described. Jessi sat on the floor, leaning over and touching her toes, with her chin practically resting on her knees — and talked to Stacey as if she were in the most comfortable position in the world. It hurt just to look at her.

At 5:29, I could see Kristy's eyes glue themselves to the clock. The instant it turned to five-thirty, she called out, "Order!"

As we quieted down, Kristy looked at the door. "Anyone know where Mallory is?"

We all shrugged.

"Orthodontist appointment?" Kristy asked Mary Anne.

Mary Anne checked the record book and shook her head. "Not till next week."

Kristy was the only one who seemed upset. I mean, everyone's human — once in awhile, just about each one of us is late.

But just try telling that to Kristy.

She let out a big sigh and said, "Okay, I have an idea for something to put in the Kid-Kits. Stacey, could you check how much money we — "

That's when Mallory came in. Now, usually when someone shows up late, she sort of quietly slips in and sits right down, mumbling "sorry" or something. But Mal didn't do that. She just stood there for a second, her brow wrinkled and her mouth in a frown. Right away we knew something was wrong.

"Mal?" Mary Anne said with concern. "Are you all right?"

Mallory gave a distracted nod. "*I'm* fine. Didn't you guys hear what happened?"

Six totally blank faces looked back at her. "No, what?" Stacey asked.

"You know the pen pals' school, in New Mexico?" she said.

We nodded.

"It burned down."

That was the last thing anyone expected to hear. We just stared at her, as if she had just said "the grass is purple," or something else you couldn't respond to.

"*What?*" Kristy finally said.

"Vanessa got a letter from her pen pal," Mal said, sitting on the edge of the bed. "There was a fire at a gas station near the school. It sort of went up like an explosion and then it spread."

"That's *horrible!*" I said.

"Was anybody hurt?" Claudia asked.

Mal shook her head. "Not seriously. But the school was destroyed, and so were some homes."

No one knew what to say. I only knew the Zuni kids through baby-sitting with the Pikes. Yet somehow, I couldn't keep my stomach from knotting up. I had listened to all the letters and, in a way, I felt that those kids were my friends, too.

"Vanessa was really upset," Mallory added, "and so were the triplets. I had to calm them down. That's why I was late."

"Wow," Stacey said in a low voice. "I wish there was something we could do."

"Maybe there is," I said.

Mallory looked at me hopefully. "What?"

I didn't know the answer to that question. But I was determined to find it.

It was a Friday night, but it sure didn't feel like it.

Usually Friday night dinner is one of the most fun times in our house. It's the beginning of the weekend and everyone's in a good mood. Sometimes there are no more leftovers and no one wants to cook, which means getting pizza or Chinese food or something. Mary Anne and I usually chatter about five miles a minute. When we're not talking, we're shoveling in food or laughing (I know this makes us sound like pigs, but we're actually neat about it).

After the BSC meeting that night, though, it was another story. Richard had picked up some vegetarian Mexican food on his way home from work, and instead of wolfing it down happily, we were all kind of quiet and lost in our thoughts.

At least I was. I was thinking about those kids in New Mexico. Mary Anne was probably thinking about them, too, but knowing her, she was also wondering why *I* was so quiet. Mom and Richard knew something was wrong, and they were trying hard to make cheerful conversation.

It was Mom who broke the ice. "Dawn," she said, "did something happen at school?"

I took a deep breath. Then I told her about Pens Across America, Conrad White, Rachel Redriver, and Sha'la'ko. I described our meeting and Mal's news about the fire. Mom listened patiently, nodding with concern. "How awful," she murmured after I'd finished.

"Maybe they didn't have a good sprinkler system," Richard added.

To be honest, that seemed like a pretty strange reaction, but I didn't say so. "I guess not," I replied with a shrug.

"I know how Dawn feels," Mary Anne said. "It just seems so . . . unfair."

"It is," I agreed. "They're really nice kids, Mom — and they work so hard, and they don't have much money . . ."

"The Pikes are really upset about it," Mary Anne added. "Mal says her brothers and sisters were almost crying. It's like something happened to their best friends."

Mom gave us both a sympathetic smile. "It

is unfair," she said. "But the important thing is that no one was seriously hurt. And they'll rebuild whatever was destroyed." She shrugged. "Life goes on."

"I just wish we could help somehow," I said.

"You can," Richard spoke up. "Maybe not the kids in New Mexico, but certainly the Pike kids — cheer them up, encourage them to write supportive letters."

"Yeah," I said, twirling a forkful of refried beans so that the melted cheese wrapped around it. "I guess you're right."

Richard *was* right, I realized. I vowed that I'd call Mal after dinner, and I started feeling a little better. The conversation picked up and things seemed to get back to normal. It was my turn to load the dishwasher that night, which took only a few minutes, since we had eaten takeout. Afterward I quickly made my call to Mal.

"Hi, Mal!" I said.

"Oh . . . hi," came Mal's voice. After we chatted a bit, she asked, "Um, now what are they going to do about the stuff they were going to send?"

"What?"

"You know, the souvenirs to the pen pals? The pennant, the decals . . ."

"Oh!" I said. "Send it all. It'll make them feel better."

"Yeah?"

"Yeah! Don't you think?"

"I don't know, it just seems a little weird. I mean, if I was one of the Zuni kids, and my house burned down, and I got a *pennant* in the mail . . . You know what I mean?"

"Oh. Yeah."

I didn't know what to say. I hadn't thought of it that way. Sending cute little souvenirs would make it seem like we weren't taking their crisis seriously. I was trying to think of something positive when Mal said, "I have to help get Claire to bed, Dawn. I'll talk to you tomorrow, okay?"

"Okay, 'bye!"

" 'Bye!"

So much for cheering up the Pikes.

I went to my room, feeling like a real jerk. I didn't have one comforting thing to say to the Pikes — but even if I did, I still wouldn't be helping the Zuni kids. One thing kept sticking in my mind: Compared to the Zunis, we were probably *rich*. Surely there had to be something the people in Stoneybrook could do. Something we could give them.

But what? And how?

I tried to imagine being one of the kids

whose homes were destroyed. What would I need right away? That was easy enough to answer: a place to sleep, food, clothes, and money.

There wasn't much I could do about the first problem. I guessed (and hoped) that the families had moved in with friends temporarily. That left food, clothes, and money — and I knew we could help out with those.

My plan began to take shape. There were three parts to it, and as I thought of each one, I got more and more excited. I talked it over with Mary Anne later that night.

She was in her room, lying on her bed, her face deep in a Judy Blume paperback I had lent her called *Tiger Eyes*.

"Guess what?" I said to her, barging in.

"Hmmm?" came her voice from behind the book.

"Mary Anne, this is important! Can I talk to you for a minute?"

"Mmm-hmm." She was still behind the book.

This was getting frustrating. "You want to know what happens to the guy in the hospital? It turns out he's really — " I started to say.

Mary Anne slammed the book. "*Dawn!* Don't spoil the ending!"

"I had to get your attention *somehow*," I said, plopping down onto her bed.

"Well, I guess *you're* in a better mood," Mary Anne said with a raised eyebrow. She sat up, curling her legs underneath her. "Okay, what's so important?"

"I know how to help the pen pals."

Suddenly Mary Anne looked interested. "Really? How?"

"It's simple! First of all, SES could have a food drive — you know, the kids go door-to-door, collecting cans and boxes, stuff that won't spoil. Then there could be a big clothing drive, and finally, some sort of fund-raiser!"

"Fund-raiser?"

"Yeah! I don't know how much money we can get, but anything's better than nothing, right?"

"Wait a minute," Mary Anne said in her practical voice. "What kind of fund-raiser?"

I shrugged. (To tell you the truth, I was kind of hoping she'd be more excited.) "I don't know, I'll figure something out. But what do you think of the *idea?*"

"It sounds great, Dawn. But it's, you know, a pretty big project. A lot of teachers will have to get involved. Do you think they'll want to do it?"

"*Sure* they will," I said confidently. "I'm not worried about that part."

"Great," Mary Anne said. I couldn't tell if she meant it, though.

The truth? I *was* worried about it. I felt like a big balloon with its air being squeezed out.

That night it took me a long time to get to sleep.

The next day, Saturday, I did something I normally would never do. I called a teacher at her home. Not only that, it was a teacher I didn't even know.

Well, I knew *of* her, actually.

Let me explain. I was excited about going to SES with my plan, but I didn't want to wait till Monday. Besides, even if I did wait, when would I get a chance to go there? Their school day is about the same as ours, so I couldn't go after school. I decided I might as well act right away. But here was the problem: Remember when I said I moved to Stoneybrook in seventh grade? You guessed it — I never went to SES, so I didn't know any teachers.

That's when I decided to call Ms. Besser. She was my brother Jeff's teacher. I probably wouldn't have remembered her name, except that Jeff used to go around the house yelling, "No more Ms. Besser!" when he was about to move to California.

Opening the phone book I felt excited, but pretty scared. I tried to imagine how I would feel if I were a teacher and some strange student called me on my day off. I didn't think

I'd mind, but adults can be funny about things like that.

Anyway, there I was, at the *B* section of the phone book. I was half hoping there were a hundred Bessers so I'd be forced to wait — or *no* Bessers. But there was only one:

BESSER, J. 555-7660

I took a deep breath and tapped out the number. By the third ring I had just about lost my nerve. I was about to hang up when a man's voice answered, "Hello?"

"Hello," I said, my mouth suddenly drying up. "Is Ms. Besser there?"

There was a short silence. "Uh, sure," the man said. Then he must have put his hand over the phone, because the next words were muffled. But I could still make them out: "Honey, it's one of your *kids!*"

Which made me feel even stranger. At first I felt a little insulted. Did I really sound that young? Then I worried that Ms. Besser wouldn't talk to me if I wasn't one of her students. *Then* I remembered what a trouble-maker Jeff had been — and I was *sure* she'd hang up the minute she heard my name!

"Hello!" came a woman's voice.

"Hi, Ms. Besser. Um, I'm Dawn Schafer. You had my brother Jeff in your class?"

"Oh, *hello*, Dawn!" (What a relief! She sounded happy.) "Yes, your mother used to talk about you. How nice to hear your voice. How's Jeff?"

I knew my mom had had conferences with Ms. Besser about Jeff, but why did they talk about *me?* I wondered. "He's really happy," I answered. "He loves California."

"Oh, that's great. I guess sending him there was a wise decision after all."

"Oh, yes, it really was." We were getting off the track, so I decided to dig right in. "Um, Ms. Besser, I wondered if I could talk to you about something."

"Of course."

"It's about the Pens Across America program. I don't know if your class is participating in it . . ."

"We are, yes." Ms. Besser was sounding curious now.

"Well, I heard about what happened — "

"Terrible, wasn't it?"

Now was my chance. "Well, that's why I was calling," I said. "I have some ideas on how to help them."

"I see."

I went over all three parts — the food drive, the clothing drive, and the fund-raiser. Ms. Besser listened silently. When she asked about the fund-raiser, I was honest and said I didn't know what it would be yet.

Without seeing her face, I couldn't tell how she felt — but she didn't exactly sound ecstatic. She let out a long "Hmmm . . ." and then said, "Sounds interesting, Dawn. I'll bring it up in the teacher's room on Monday."

I was dying to know how she felt, but I didn't want to come right out and ask. So I said, "Do you think they might go for it?"

"Well, if *I* have any say in it, they will," she answered. "I mean, after all, what's the point of a pen pal program? They're supposed to be *pals*, right?"

"Right," I agreed.

"And if I allow my kids to let down their friends, I'm not doing my job, right?"

"Right!"

"What's your number, Dawn? I'll call you Monday evening and let you know what happens. If the idea goes over, we'll talk about how to organize it."

I was so thrilled, I could barely get my own phone number straight. When I hung up, I let out a whoop of joy. Imagine me, Dawn Schafer, organizing a huge help campaign. It was like something Kristy might do.

Kristy.

Suddenly I realized something that would

make my idea even better. Why not get Kristy interested? This would make a perfect project for the whole BSC.

So I called her. Lucky for me, she was home. And when I told her my plan, her reaction was exactly as I would have predicted.

"We have to have an emergency meeting as soon as you hear from Ms. Besser," she said. "We have to figure out what the fund-raising drive is going to be, where and when we're going to have all these things, how we can get the kids excited — all that kind of stuff."

"It'll be fun!" I said.

"Yup," Kristy answered. "Be sure to call me right away, okay?"

"Okay."

It was typical Kristy — taking charge. I was glad but a little uncomfortable. Kristy meant well, but I hoped she wasn't going to make it seem like it was *her* idea.

Hey, ease up, I told myself. The important thing was helping the kids, not taking credit for it.

Well, it turned out that the SES teachers were really enthusiastic about the idea. Ms. Besser didn't even wait to call me at home. One of the assistant principals at *our* school found me during lunch period and said that

Ms. Besser had called and asked him to tell me the plan was on.

I hope he didn't think I was rude when I yelled "yea!" and ran off to find Kristy.

By the end of the school day, Kristy had contacted everyone in the Baby-sitters Club. Our Monday night meeting was to start a half hour early, at five o'clock. We were going to plan Operation Help.

I got to Claudia's fifteen minutes early. I was so excited I couldn't even think of eating snacks. Besides, I spent the whole time talking to Claud about my plan. One by one, the others arrived. Mary Anne informed us that Jessi and Stacey had baby-sitting jobs right up to the regular meeting time, but by 4:58, everyone else was there.

I could feel my heart racing as Kristy called out, "Order!"

As it turned out, I didn't need to worry about Kristy taking credit for my idea. This is the way she opened the meeting:

"Okay, some of you know why this special meeting has been called. But for those who don't, I'll let Dawn explain." She turned to me. "Dawn?"

I was happy to be the one with the big idea for once. And everyone listened carefully as I explained my plan.

Mal was especially excited. "Are we going to vote on this?" she asked when I'd finished speaking. "I vote yes."

"I vote yes," Mary Anne added.

"Me, too!" Claudia said.

Kristy cut them off. "Wait a minute! Is there a motion to put this to a vote?"

Claudia groaned. In a weary, impatient voice, she said, "I motion we put this to a vote."

"Put *what* to a vote?" Kristy said. "You have to be specific."

"*Kristy!*" Claudia said, rolling her eyes. "I motion that we vote whether the Baby-sitters Club should help out with Dawn's plan, okay?"

"Seconds?" Kristy said.

"I second the motion," Mary Anne called out.

"All those in favor, raise your hands," Kristy said.

Everyone's hand shot in the air.

"It's unanimous," Kristy announced.

"Yea, Dawn!" Mal exclaimed.

"Great," I said. "I'll call Ms. Besser and ask her to tell her students."

"And I'll get my brothers and sisters to tell their teachers," Mallory added.

"That's still not enough," Kristy said. "There are four whole grades, and each grade has a lot of classes . . ."

"How about making a flier?" I suggested. "Ms. Besser could make copies, then we could post it around the school."

"I'll make it!" Claudia chimed in. She took a drawing pad off her night table. "Okay . . . what should I put in this?"

"Who, what, when, where, why," Kristy recited. "*Who* is all the kids in the Pens Across America program."

"*What* is a door-to-door food-and-clothing drive," I said. "All canned goods, dry goods, old clothes, shoes — "

"The clothes should be clean," Mary Anne said. "We should mention that."

"Clean clothes," I agreed. "*Why* is the fire at the Zuni reservation."

"The *tragic* fire," Claudia added.

"*When* is something we have to ask the teachers about," Mal added.

"Where's *where*?" Kristy asked.

"What?" Claudia said.

"Where," Kristy repeated.

"Where's what?" Mary Anne said.

I started giggling. I couldn't help it. It was beginning to sound like a comedy routine.

"Where's *where*?" Kristy said. "I mean, *where* should the kids bring the clothing and the food? They have to drop it off someplace."

"We can use my barn," I said. "I'll ask Mom and Richard. I'm sure they won't mind."

"Great," Claudia said. "I'll pencil it in."

"I have an idea," Mallory said. "If we really want to get kids excited about this stuff, we should have prizes or awards — "

"Or maybe a big party for everyone who participates," Mary Anne said. "That way it's not so competitive."

Mallory nodded. "You mean, like a school picnic."

"I heard of a school where the kids became teachers for a day," Kristy said. "That might be fun."

Then I had a great idea. "How about a big sleepover?" I said. "We could use the gym, and maybe some of the school staff could participate."

"I like that," Claudia said. "Can you imagine, all those little kids in pajamas?"

The whole night was taking shape in my mind. "We can serve pizza for dinner," I said, "then afterwards maybe organize some games — you know, a basketball shooting contest, a singalong — "

"Red Rover," Mal added.

"I Spy," Claudia said.

"Right," I said. "If we wanted to hand out awards, we could have a ceremony. Let's see. We'll ask the kids to bring sleeping bags, and maybe we can use rubber mats as mattresses. In the morning we'll make pancakes or something — it'll be so much fun!"

"Yeah," Kristy said, nodding. "And also not too expensive, aside from the food."

"Maybe we can ask a pizza place to donate pies for the cause," I said.

"We could try," Kristy replied. "All right, all in favor of the sleepover?"

Again everyone raised hands. Mal raised two.

"Okay, that's that," Kristy said.

"I'll mention it in the flier," Claudia said.

Suddenly Kristy looked deep in thought. "Wait a minute, I just thought of something. Do you really think a lot of kids'll read the fliers?"

"Oops . . ." Mal said. "Some of them can barely read."

"We have to make sure they *all* know," Kristy said.

"We should notify parents, too, right?" Mary Anne said. "And what about the rest of Stoneybrook? So it won't be a total surprise when kids come knocking on doors."

"Oh . . ." I said, trying to think of answers.

"And what about the fund-raiser?" Kristy said. "We never decided exactly how the kids are going to earn money."

Everyone stopped talking for awhile. You could almost hear the thoughts tumbling around inside our heads.

Finally Mal said, "I think we should let them come up with their own ways."

"But they're just *kids*," Claudia said.

"My brothers and sisters are just kids, too," Mal said. "But remember what they did when our dad lost his job?"

"That's right," Claudia said with a smile. "I'll never forget Vanessa styling kids' hair on the school playground."

"And Nicky's paper route," I said, "and that 'company' the triplets created for doing odd jobs in the neighborhood."

"They really managed to pull it together," Mal said.

The phone rang, just as Jessi and Stacey raced into the room. I'd almost forgotten where we were — and what time it was.

Five thirty-two. The special meeting was officially over. Claudia grabbed the receiver. "Hello, Baby-sitters Club," she said. "Oh, hi, Mrs. Braddock! . . . Uh-huh . . . just a minute, let me check."

For the next half hour, we were pretty busy making appointments and juggling schedules. We never did resolve all of Kristy's questions that afternoon.

But still, I was incredibly excited. It would be a ton of work, but my plan was going to become a reality.

Wednesday

Dawn, your idea is fantastic! I was so excited after Monday's meeting, I wanted to blurt it out to everyone. It was really hard to keep it a secret that night when I baby-sat for Charlotte Johanssen. But then I had to sit for her again last night, and you know what happened.

Anyway, there's one thing you need to know about Charlotte. Her new favorite books are the "Freddy the Pig" series (be prepared - she's addicted to them). She's been talking about them endlessly, but last night she started talking about her pen pal. The rest is history. I never would have thought Char would be the one to solve our problem - except, knowing her, I shouldn't have been so surprised....

In case you're wondering what Stacey meant, let me explain.

Charlotte Johanssen is really smart. She's eight, but she was skipped into fourth grade. Charlotte used to be quiet and shy, but gradually, she's become more outgoing and talkaative.

There were two reasons for the change in Charlotte. Number One: skipping the grade, which made school more interesting for her (she was bored to tears before). Number Two: Stacey! She and Charlotte have gotten really close, and Dr. Johanssen (Char's mom) says that Stacey helped bring Charlotte out of her shell.

That Monday *and* Tuesday, both Johanssens were busy (Char's mom had to do emergency-room shifts at Stoneybrook General Hospital, and her dad had to work late on an engineering project), and Stacey got both sitting jobs.

Tuesday evening, Charlotte figured out something that none of us could — a way to make sure *all* of the SES kids knew about my plan.

The evening started out normally. Charlotte was showing Stacey how her body language could affect Carrot, the Johanssens' schnauzer.

Carrot was sitting by the fireplace, lazily

looking around the living room. Charlotte and Stacey were on the couch. "Now watch," Charlotte said. She let her shoulders slump, she pouted her lips, and she let her hair fall in front of her face.

Carrot cocked his head to the side, then trotted toward Charlotte. When he began licking her face, Charlotte laughed. "You are *such* a smart doggy!" she said. "You want a — "

Without finishing the sentence, she stood up as if she were going to run to the kitchen.

Carrot yelped happily and sprinted into the kitchen.

"See?" Charlotte said, smiling. "I didn't have to say anything!"

"That's great, Char," Stacey said as they followed Carrot.

Charlotte got Carrot a few dog biscuits, then said, "I'm starving, Stace. Can we have a snack, *please?*"

"So *that's* why you got Carrot to come in here," Stacey said with a laugh. "Well, all right. Your mom said we could have a few pretzels, but that's it."

Charlotte made a face. "You mean those hard ones with no salt?"

"Those are the only ones in here," Stacey said, pulling out a bag that said PRETZELS AU NATUREL — LOW SODIUM. "Besides, there's salt *in* them, just not *on* them."

"Oh," Charlotte said. She took a pretzel from the bag and plopped down in a kitchen chair.

Stacey sat across from her and placed the open bag on the table, next to a neat stack of yellow, lined paper and envelopes. Judging from the big, scrawly, fourth-graderish handwriting, Stacey figured they were letters from Charlotte's pen pal, whose name was Theresa Bradley. "Have you heard from Theresa?"

"Mm-hm," Charlotte said with her mouth closed. The pretzel crunched loudly as she chewed. Then she swallowed and said, "Her house caught fire."

"Oh, that's *terrible,*" Stacey said. "Is she all right?"

Charlotte nodded. "You want to read the letter?" She took the top sheet off the stack and handed it to Stacey.

"Thanks," Stacey said. She read aloud:

" 'Dear Charlotte,

" 'I really liked your letter. I didn't read any Freddy books yet. You know what happened? There was this big, huge fire! It started at this gas station, then it burned our school down! Our house was on fire, too. I couldn't believe it! We are okay because we were outside. My dad and my uncles got fire extinguishers. They sprayed inside the house. The fire went out, but a lot of things were burned. Now our house is being fixed. We have to live with my aunt and uncle's family. My aunt was a teacher at the school and she lost her job.

" 'Some of my clothes were in the washing machine. Those didn't get burned. I wear them every day now. Our TV and VCR burned, too. My aunt and uncle have a TV but not a VCR.

" 'Things aren't too bad. Sometimes it's fun to have so many people around. But my brother wakes up with nightmares sometimes, and my grandmother and my mom cry a lot.

" 'My cousin says we're lucky. She's in high school. She wishes her school burned. My mom got mad when she heard this. She said our education is the most important thing we have. I don't think we're lucky, either. I miss school.

" 'Write me back at my aunt and uncle's house. I wrote the address on the envelope. 'Bye.

" 'Your friend, Theresa.' "

Well, Stacey's heart just about broke as she read the letter. (Mine did, too, when she told us about it at the Wednesday meeting.)

"Isn't that sad?" Charlotte said.

Stacey nodded. "Yeah, it really is."

Char's brow was wrinkled, the way it gets when she's upset about something. "What would happen if my house burned, Stacey?"

"Oh, Char, you don't need to worry about that — "

"Could we move in with you?"

Stacey didn't know what to say. "Well, I guess — sure, I mean, Mom would — "

"Because we don't have aunts and uncles in Stoneybrook, and I don't want to move away. I would be so lonely."

Charlotte was fiddling nervously with her pretzel, so Stacey reached out to touch her hands. "It's okay, Charlotte. Nothing like that is going to happen."

That's when Stacey decided to tell her about my plan — even though we had all promised not to tell anyone until we actually got started. Stacey figured it might help Charlotte feel better. (Later on, we all agreed she did the right thing.)

"Char," she began. "Can you keep a secret?"

Charlotte perked up. "A secret? About what?"

"Well . . ." Stacey leaned forward and lowered her voice, sounding mysterious. "Dawn thought up this plan to help your pen pals. Only the members of the Baby-sitters Club know about it. We want everyone in your school to be in a food-and-clothing drive — you know, going door-to-door and collecting stuff to send to your friends. We're also going to ask kids to try to raise money on their own. Do you think that's a good idea?"

Charlotte's eyes lit up. "Yeah! When — "

"Wait. I didn't tell you the best part. There's going to be a humongous sleepover in the SES gym for everyone who helps out."

"Wow! That is *so* fantastic!"

"But don't tell anybody," Stacey said. "We want to figure out a good way to spread the word fast — to the school, the parents, the whole town!"

"Ooh! Are you going to have a big assembly?"

"Well, something like that — " Stacey cut herself off. She couldn't believe none of *us* had thought of an assembly.

"That would be so much fun, Stacey!" Charlotte went on. "You guys can announce it to the whole school, then we'll tell our friends and parents. And our parents can tell *their* friends."

Stacey grinned. "Char, you are amazing. I can't wait to tell Dawn."

"Really?" Charlotte said, beaming.

"No. I have a better idea. Since you thought of it, why don't *you* tell Dawn? We can ride over to her house right now."

"Okay!" Charlotte ran to the garage while Stacey wrote a note to the Johanssens, in case one of them came back early. Then Stacey followed Charlotte out, closing the door behind her.

Char was already on her bike, and Stacey had ridden hers to the Johanssens', so she hopped on it. "Okay," she said, "let's go, but be careful." (Once a baby-sitter, always a baby-sitter.)

Stacey rode down the driveway and onto Kimball Street, ahead of Charlotte. They pedaled fast, making the ride to Burnt Hill Road in about five minutes (at least that's what Stacey said, but I think she was exaggerating).

Mary Anne and I were both home. Let me tell you, I have never seen Charlotte so excited. Once, when the younger girls were all involved in a beauty pageant, Charlotte was too nervous to recite a section of *Charlie and the Chocolate Factory* for the talent competition. You would never know this was the same person.

"Char, that's a *perfect* solution," I said, and I meant it. "I'll talk to Ms. Besser and set up the assembly."

"For when?" Mary Anne said. "We all have to be in school, remember?"

"It won't take that long," I replied. "We'll just have to get permission to leave for a little while."

"You think you can?" Charlotte asked hopefully.

"Yup," I said. (Even though I wasn't a *hundred* percent positive, I was pretty sure we could convince our teachers.)

We talked about it a little longer, until Stacey decided it was time to leave. She said that Charlotte kept chattering about the assembly right up until her mom came home, but then she kept the secret and didn't say a word.

Stacey could tell Charlotte was much happier — and not only that, she was probably going to be a big help with our project.

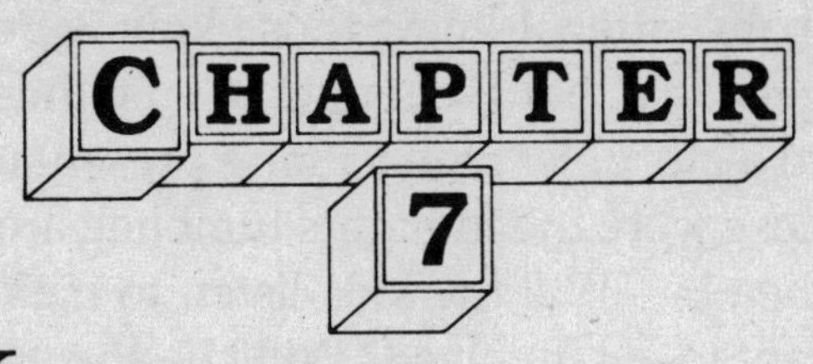

"Kristin Reinhardt?"

"Here."

"Jodi Reynolds?"

"Present."

"Nicole Rogers?"

"Here."

I could barely hear my homeroom teacher, Mr. Blake, reading the role call. My brain felt like it was spinning in my head. It was Friday, the day we were going to have our assembly at SES.

Are you surprised at how fast it happened? I was. I had only talked to Ms. Besser about the assembly on Wednesday. Then she spoke to the SES principal, who arranged everything. At ten-fifteen on Friday, all the second-, third-, fourth-, and fifth-grade classes were going to meet in the school auditorium.

To hear me!

That's right — since it was my plan, I was

supposed to tell them about it. I don't mind giving school reports or talking in front of a class, but this was really making me nervous. I mean, *four whole grades!* And as an experienced baby-sitter, I knew those kids were not all angels. It's hard enough to get them to listen to a story, let alone a long presentation.

So these were the thoughts tumbling around in my head — Will the kids listen to me? Will they want to get involved? Will I be so nervous that I say something stupid?

For about the tenth time, I reached into my shoulder bag to make sure the speech I had written was still there.

I didn't even hear when Mr. Blake called my name.

I snapped back to reality when I felt Mary Anne nudge me (she sits behind me in homeroom). Then I heard Ray Stuckey, the class clown, saying, "Earth to Dawn! Earth to Dawn!"

A few people laughed, but I was too nervous to be embarrassed. "Here!" I said quickly.

Mr. Blake went on with the roll call, until he was interrupted by the intercom.

"Attention, please. This is Mr. Taylor speaking."

Mr. Taylor is the principal of the Stoneybrook Middle School. He speaks very slowly, and whenever I hear his voice over the intercom, I feel like going to sleep.

But not this time. This time I knew he was going to be talking about me.

"The following students will be dismissed at five minutes to ten," Mr. Taylor went on. "Claudia Kishi, Stacey McGill, Mallory Pike, Jessica Ramsey, Dawn Schafer, Mary Anne Spier, and Kristy Thomas. All teachers please be advised."

When I turned to look at Mary Anne, she had a big, excited grin on her face. She didn't look nervous at all. Why should she? *She* wasn't the one who had to do the talking.

"Well, excuuuuse *me!*" Ray said under his breath. "If *I* join the Baby-sitters Club, will I get a day off, too?"

"Mr. Stuckey!" Mr. Blake's voice boomed out.

"Eat your heart out, Ray," I whispered. That is *not* something I would normally say, but I was feeling so keyed up, I couldn't help it.

Homeroom ended, then came math class and boring, *boring* algebraic equations. I looked at the *x*'s and *y*'s and thought I was reading ancient Greek. I could have sworn the clock on the wall was running at half speed.

The exact moment the clock read 9:55, I raised my hand. Ms. Berner, my teacher, nodded at me and said, "Good luck."

I guess the news had spread to the SMS teachers, too. That made me feel even *more* nervous — like there was this big audience waiting to hear how I did.

I ran outside, where Ms. Downey, the school secretary, was waiting in a station wagon. "Thanks for doing this," I said to her.

"Don't mention it," she said, smiling. "I'm *thrilled* to get away from that computer screen for an hour!"

As I got in the front seat, I heard "Hey, Dawn!" and I looked out the window to see Claudia and Mary Anne running out the school entrance.

Kristy and Stacey followed close behind, then Mal and Jessi. They all piled in — Mary Anne next to me; Claudia, Kristy, and Stacey in the backseat; and Mal and Jessi in the back of the station wagon.

We were off. I don't remember much about the trip to the elementary school. I was too busy trying to control the flutter in my stomach and the tingle in my fingertips. (I can't imagine how an actor must feel. Like this? And if so, how come actors always look so relaxed?)

The SES parking lot was pretty full, so Ms. Downey dropped us off at a back entrance. There, Ms. Besser was waiting.

"Hi!" she said cheerfully. "You must be Dawn. You look just like your brother."

I don't think so, but everyone says I do. Anyway, I think I nodded and said "Thanks," or something else meaningless.

"I'm so glad you girls are doing this," Ms. Besser went on, leading us inside. "The kids will be really excited about it."

We walked through the school cafeteria, which was empty and smelled like overboiled broccoli. Then we entered a long corridor.

"My class is already there, along with a couple of others," Ms. Besser said over her shoulder to us.

That's when I could hear the noise coming from the auditorium — it was like a playground, only with an echo. Every few seconds, a weary adult voice shouted out, "Turn around, Justin!" or "All right, keep it down!"

Suddenly I wished I had never thought of this plan. I wanted to turn and run.

I looked at my friends and noticed they were all looking at me. Mary Anne quickly took my hand and squeezed it. "You're going to be great!" she said.

I took a deep breath and followed Ms. Besser through a door that led to the backstage of the auditorium. Ms. Reynolds, the SES principal, was waiting for us there. She has red hair and a strong, kind face. I liked her right away. Shaking our hands warmly, she said, "Is there anything you need?"

Everyone sort of stared blankly, until I replied, "No, I think we're just going to talk."

She nodded. "This was a very smart idea, you know."

"Thanks," I said again. My voice sounded squeaky.

Behind us was a curtain that hid the audience from us. Ms. Besser had walked around it and onto the stage. Now she reappeared, saying, "They're almost all here. Are you ready?"

Feeling numb, I nodded.

Mary Anne squeezed my hand again as Ms. Besser walked back onstage, saying, "Okay, quiet please! Take your seats!"

As soon as the kids quieted down, we followed Ms. Reynolds onto the stage. There was a podium with a microphone in the center of it. Behind the podium were nine chairs, arranged in a semicircle. Ms. Reynolds gestured for us to sit down.

We did, and I made the mistake of looking into the audience. I felt that a million pairs of little eyes were staring at our every movement. There was a lump in my throat the size of a basketball.

It's amazing how loud an auditorium full of

kids can be, even when no one's actually saying anything. All the fidgeting, sighing, coughing, hiccuping, burping, switching seats — it's never *completely* silent.

Ms. Reynolds walked to the podium. "Good morning," she began. "When we called this a special assembly, we really meant *special*. These girls are familiar to some of you. They have something in common with *all* of you — they care about the children in your sister school in Zuni, New Mexico."

Now the kids *really* quieted down. Ms. Reynolds went on a little while, then said, "Now, these girls have school, too, so they'll have to leave right after the assembly. If you have any questions later on, you can ask Ms. Besser." Ms. Besser, who was sitting with us, stood up and smiled. "Now I'd like to introduce you to the mastermind of the plan. She'll fill you in on all the details. Here's Dawn Schafer!"

I was on. As I stepped up to the podium, clutching my speech, I didn't feel much of anything. I caught a glimpse of Vanessa Pike, grinning widely. Ms. Reynolds had adjusted the mike downward, but I had to adjust it some more. It made a loud *scrawwwk*, and some of the kids laughed.

"Hi, everybody," I said. The sound of my own voice startled me. It boomed out from the speakers on the auditorium walls, and it sounded high-pitched and mumbly and *awful!*

"Hi, Dawn!" came a voice from the back. I was pretty sure it was Haley Braddock, and I smiled.

"Um, first I'd like to introduce my friends behind me," I said, turning around. "Next to Ms. Besser is Mary Anne Spier . . ."

Ms. Besser said something to Mary Anne, and she stood up. Her face was redder than I'd ever seen it.

"Yea, Mary Anne!" That was a different voice. There was some applause, too.

One by one I introduced the BSC members. Occasionally I heard a cheer from the crowd. I was beginning to loosen up. Obviously, we had some fans. (Which made sense, considering all the baby-sitting hours we'd put in!)

Then I began reading from my speech. I mentioned how concerned we were about the Zuni kids, and how the fire had put people out of homes and jobs. At one point I heard a huge, loud yawn. When I looked up, a teacher was pulling a boy up the aisle by his right hand. A few other kids laughed.

Great. I was *boring* them.

I decided to look up from my speech to tell them about the plan by heart. (Hey, if I didn't know it well enough by now, I was in bad shape.) Sure enough, I didn't make any mistakes. As I outlined the food drive, the clothing drive, and the fund-raising, I could see everyone just looking at me. When I urged the kids to spread the word about our project, I could see a few heads nodding.

And you know what? I was beginning to feel confident. I could tell the kids were interested.

Of course, I saved the best for last. "This is all going to be a lot of work," I said. "And it's always nice to get a reward when you work hard, right?"

A couple of kids answered, "Right!"

"I think your biggest reward will be knowing that you helped your friends," I went on. "But we would like to give you a celebration of your own. Whoever participates in the drive will get to go to a slumber party in the school gym — with food, games, storytelling, contests, you name it!"

Well, all of a sudden they became *kids* again. Some of them bounced in their seats and clapped. Others let out squeals and began talking to their neighbors. Still others raised their hands, as if we were about to *pick* people to go to the sleepover.

A few of the teachers had to shush some kids. I looked at my watch. My speech was over, but I realized we still had five minutes to go. "Um, does anybody have any questions?"

Haley's hand shot up. "Haley?" I said.

"That's the best idea I ever heard, Dawn!" she blurted out. "Can we tell our pen pals what we're doing?"

"I'm glad you asked that," I said. "The answer is no. This is going to be a surprise. If you write to them, don't even give the slightest hint."

Then I called on Valerie Namm, a friend of Charlotte's, whose hand was raised. "Valerie?"

"How long will the drive last?" she asked.

"About three weeks," I said. "Longer if it's going really well."

The next person I called on was David Michael, Kristy's brother. "When we go to people's houses, can we collect money, too?" he asked.

I looked back at the other BSC members. They were all leaning over to Kristy, who stood up and said, "Sure. Since fund-raising is going to be up to you, that can be *your* method."

"Rob," I said, pointing to Rob Hines.

"Can we just go to the party and forget the other stuff?" he asked.

Three or four boys on either side of him began to laugh.

"No work, no play," I answered.

Then I called on Jordan Pike.

"Hey, Mal," he said, "what's that thing crawling up the wall behind you?"

Mal spun around, and *Jordan's* group of friends began to howl with laughter. That's when Ms. Besser stood up and said, "All right, if you have any more questions — *real* questions — I'll take them for the next few minutes. But first let's have a round of applause for the girls before they leave!"

The kids did applaud — enthusiastically, too. As I led the other BSC members off the stage, I waved to the kids. When we got to the hallway, we all did a little jumping and squealing and giggling of our own.

Inside, through the open door, we could hear Ms. Besser answering more questions.

"You did it, Dawn!" Kristy said, beaming.

"I guess," I said. I was trying not to get overexcited, because there was *so* much work to do now. But the truth was, I felt like shouting with joy. The assembly was a success, and we were on our way!

Monday

Well, this doesn't have anything to do with baby-sitting, really.

Yes it does, Mal. Mal thinks that taking care of thirty-five kids doesn't count as baby-sitting!

I know, Jessi, but this was a carnival. It's a different story. Anyway, it doesn't matter. I was going to write about it, baby-sitting or not. I think we did a great job, and we ended up raising a lot of money. If it weren't for Goober Mansfield...

I knew you were going to write about him first. You should start with the good things!

He was good!

Mal, he ruined the whole day. And it was all my fault.

That's not true. Okay, okay, I know that look in your eyes. Maybe you should write about it.

I'd be happy to. Let's see, it all began at about 10:00 on Saturday morning . . .

That Saturday was exactly one week and a day after the assembly at SES. Mal and Jessi had somehow managed to organize a carnival in the Pikes' backyard. Booths, grab bags, a magic show, the works.

Now, carnivals are supposed to be a little wild, but this one . . . well, let's just say things didn't go the way anyone had expected.

It started out great. Every day that week, Mal and Jessi got together and planned all the details with the younger Pike kids and some of their friends. They built stands out of cardboard boxes and used a lot of old stuff the Pikes had around the house. For whatever else they needed, they pooled money with Mal's brothers and sisters.

The kids had plenty of ideas for the carnival. Mr. Pike had just put up a basketball hoop on the garage, so Adam and Byron set up a free-throw contest. (It cost a quarter to try, so I don't know why they called it "*free* throw." All I know is when I asked them, they rolled their eyes as if I were really stupid.)

Nicky and Jordan made a grab bag out of a huge duffel bag, which they stuffed with little prizes like pencils and baseball cards and comic books. Vanessa and Margo took a plastic wading pool and made a "fishing pond." They used Claire's rubber ducks, Lack, Mack, Nack, Ouack, Pack, and Quack (named after the ducks in *Make Way for Ducklings*). If you could pick up one of the ducks, using a fishing rod with a big plastic hook, you could win a small prize.

Jessi had invited her cousin Keisha to come up from New Jersey for the weekend to help out. The two of them took Polaroid pictures of people in a pretty spot in front of the Pikes' garden, for a fee. (Whenever they didn't have customers, Jessi went around taking candid shots, which sold really well, too.) Marilyn and Carolyn Arnold, who are twins, organized a ringtoss, using plastic bowling pins. David Michael Thomas made plastic name tags and messages for people, using one of those little rotating things that look like mini versions of the Starship *Enterprise*. Linny Papadakis, David Michael's friend, performed a magic show. The audience entered his "theater" through a "curtain," which was a couple of strung-up blankets that blocked off a corner of the yard.

So, there the kids were, ten o'clock Saturday morning, frantically setting up. There was a steady *slap, slap, slap . . . bonk!* as Adam and Jordon dribbled and shot baskets on the driveway (and missed most of the time — the *bonk!* was the ball hitting the rim). Linny, wearing a shiny fake handlebar mustache and a long black cape, was standing outside his curtains and practicing his sales pitch. "Come one, come all, to the greatest magic show on earth!" he shouted over and over. You would not believe the chaos in the yard.

Oh, well, it was for a good cause, right?

Jessi was making sure the garden looked nice, tossing away dead flowers and stray toys that were lying around. Mal was running all over the place, checking the booths. She spotted Vanessa having trouble blowing up the wading pool. "Vanessa," she called out, "why don't you get Dad or Mom to help — "

All of a sudden she was hit from the right. She stumbled, then looked over to see Adam running across the yard. The basketball was heading for Linny's curtains. "If you guys can't control the ball, I'm not going to let you have your contest!" Mal shouted.

"You can't say that," Jordan snapped back. "You don't even have a pen pal!"

Mal was trying to figure out the logic of that when Jessi leaped in front of her and said, "Say cheese!"

"Jessi, don't!" Mal said, but it was too late. Jessi snapped the shutter, and the picture came shooting out the front of the camera.

As they watched it develop, Mal groaned. Her eyes were half shut and her lips were curled in a weird, snarly way. "Ew!" she said. "Throw it out!"

"I *told* you to say 'cheese,' " Jessi said.

"Oh, never mind," Mal said. "Did you talk to Boober yet?"

Overhearing, Claire squealed, "Boober the *Fraggle* is coming?"

"Goober," Jessi corrected them. "He's going to do three shows — at twelve, two, and four."

"Good," Mal said. "We'll set him up in the driveway."

"Oh, no you won't!" came Adam's voice. "*We* need it!"

"The shows aren't long," Mal said. "Besides, I don't want anybody shooting dumb baskets while the show is on."

"Everybody'll be watching him, anyway," Jessi added.

You must be dying to know who Goober

Mansfield is. His real name is Peter, and he's the star of all the high school plays in a nearby town called Mercer. He's even had a part in a professional theater production of *Shenandoah*. Jessi found out about him in ballet class. One of her classmates, Julie Mansfield, is Goober's cousin. Julie mentioned that Goober did a dinosaur show at parties in Mercer, and all the kids there loved it.

Well, Jessi got a call from him that night. He was so enthusiastic — and funny — that she signed him up.

He showed up at the Pikes' in a minivan around ten-thirty the day of the carnival. Mal liked him right away. He had a round face with a goony smile, and a loose, rubbery body. Just seeing him made her want to laugh. You know how a person sometimes resembles a name? Well, he sort of *looked* like a Goober.

He and two of his brothers pulled a heavy wooden trunk out of the minivan. Mal led them into the yard and pointed to the driveway. "Set up over there, next to the basketball hoop."

"*Mal* — " Adam began to protest, but Mal gave him a Look.

Adam and Jordan sulked as Goober began setting up. He pulled out a papier-mâché tyrannosauraus head, a pair of big dinosaur feet made from diving flippers, a couple of strange-looking masks, a portable cassette player, and a bullhorn.

Right around then, Claire raced up the driveway, shouting, "They're coming!"

"Who?" Mal asked.

"People!" Claire said, jumping up and down.

There were shrieks of excitement (from the booths that were prepared) and panic (from the ones that weren't). Everyone hurried around, doing last-minute things.

"Okay!" Mal called out above the noise. "Get ready!"

Then, finally, it began.

The first to arrive were Linny Papadakis's parents and two sisters. They, of course, went straight to the magic show. A few minutes later, Betsy Sobak and her parents came, then the Prezziosos.

Before long, the yard was full. Mal guided kids to the booths. Jessi and Keisha snapped away. Goober moved his stuff far enough from the basketball hoop for Adam and Jordan to have their contest. Linny had a steady stream of customers in the magic booth.

At exactly noon, a whistle blew shrilly.

Mal quickly looked at her watch. "Oh! It's time for the show!" She cleared her throat and called out, "Attention every — "

"Awroooooo!" She couldn't even finish the sentence before Goober began shouting into a bullhorn. "I am a giant duck-bill dinosaur!" he shouted. "Please help me, I'm dying! *Hellllllllp meee! Awrooooo!"*

He was wearing a scary mask that looked something like the Creature from the Black Lagoon, plus green flipper feet. He wriggled and twisted as if he were in great pain, then fell to his knees. "Helllp meee!"

Kids quickly finished their games. One by one, they gathered around Goober and watched, fascinated. Suddenly he stopped yelling and cocked his head. Then he sprang to his feet and roared.

A couple of the kids screamed gleefully, and Goober began laughing. "There, that'th better!" he said in a goofy, lisping voice that reminded Mal of the Cowardly Lion in *The Wizard of Oz*. "What kinda dinothaur would I be if I couldn't thcare people?"

In no time, everyone was watching. Even Adam and Jordan put down their basketballs and stared. Goober impersonated different dinosaurs, talking about their characteristics, when they lived, whether they ate plants or meat, things like that. He even performed an original dinosaur rap song, dressed as a stegosaurus.

When Mal told me about the show, I wished I'd seen it — but mostly because of what happened later.

It was during the second show that the Perkins family arrived. (They live in Kristy's old house, and they're regular customers of ours.) Many of the kids there had already seen the first show, so all the exhibits were busy. Gabbie Perkins, who's almost three, came racing into the backyard with a tennis ball, giggling. Beside her was their Labrador retriever, Chewy (short for Chewbacca).

"Ugh! Is *that* what took over after we became extinct?" Goober's voice boomed out.

Gabbie spun around to see Goober, wearing his tyrannosaurus mask and pointing at Chewy.

Everyone watching the show turned around. Goober took a step toward Chewie.

Gabbie looked half interested, half frightened — but Chewy knew exactly how he felt. He drew back his lips and let out a snarl.

"Say, pal," Goober said in a deep, rough voice. "How'd a little thing like *you* end up surviving to the twentieth century?"

With that, he leaned down to pet Chewy.

Well, maybe it was that big, ugly mask, or maybe Goober looked like he was attacking, but Chewy did something no one had ever seen him do before.

He turned tail and ran.

"Chewy!" Gabbie cried out.

"Chewy, *no!*" called Myriah, her older sister.

It turned out that Jamie Newton was a little afraid of dogs — and a *lot* afraid of dogs who jumped in front of him without warning.

Jamie's shriek was practically bloodcurdling. He ran away — right into Marilyn and Carolyn's ringtoss. Their bowling pins went flying.

Marilyn ran after the pins. Mrs. Newton ran after Jamie. Myriah and Gabbie ran after Chewy.

And Chewy decided to run into Linny's curtains to hide. He plunged right in, snapping them off the clothesline.

The three kids watching the magic show stood up in surprise. So did Linny.

"Hey, you're ruining my act!" Linny shouted.

"Chewy!" Gabbie said.

"Waaaaah!" Jamie cried.

Jessi was mortified. She ran to Jamie's side as Mal helped Marilyn, Carolyn, and Linnie.

It didn't take long to get everything back to normal. Jamie recovered and went home. Mr. Perkins took Chewy back to his house. The exhibits were fixed up and Goober continued his show.

It did take awhile for Jessi and Mal to recover. For a long time they talked about Goober Mansfield as if he had ruined the day. But Jessi realized one important thing. After all that crazy stuff had happened, the carnival became twice as crowded.

Maybe, despite everything, Goober Mansfield was the best thing that happened that day.

monday

Yestirday was the yard sail at the Rudowskis. Boy was I glad to read about youre carnavel, Jesi. Dont get me rong Its just maks me feel beter, that I wasnt the only one who had a tough time. Remeber when I was assined to supervize the sale and I said that if Jacky Rudousky was involvd it was bound to be a disastr? Well the funy thing was, it wasn't even Jacky who mest up.

Claudia's story actually started a week before she wrote her entry. At our meeting the Monday after the assembly, she picked up a call from Mrs. Rodowsky.

"Hi, Mrs. Rodowsky," she said. "Can we help you?"

I hate to say it, but you could practically hear us thinking "Oh, no!"

I should tell you one thing. Sitting for Jackie Rodowsky is only for the very brave. He is the most accident-prone seven-year-old you've ever met. If there's food on the table, chances are he'll spill it. If there's something on the ground, chances are he'll trip over it. If he has a new outfit on, you can bet there'll be a rip in it by the end of the day. Claudia always wears her most indestructible clothes when she sits for the Rodowskys. If she had a suit of armor, that would probably be better.

"Jackie and Shea were telling me about the plan you girls are organizing," Mrs. Rodowsky said, "and Jackie had the most wonderful idea — a yard sale. We can get families to donate things they don't need anymore. I'd be happy to volunteer my backyard. And I was wondering if one of you could supervise the sale."

"Oh," Claudia said, trying to sound enthusiastic but imagining Jackie toppling over a table full of china, "that's a great — "

"How does Sunday sound?" Mrs. Rodowsky continued. "Do you think that gives us enough time?"

"Uh, sure, I think so," Claudia said. "Let me talk it over with everyone. We'll be . . . happy to help you."

"Great. I'll have the boys spread the word in school, and I'll contact their teachers. We'll talk later in the week about details."

"Okay," Claudia said.

"Terrific. 'Bye, Claudia."

" 'Bye."

Well, no one exactly jumped out of her seat to volunteer to be in charge. In fact, we actually had to choose straws. And of course, Claud picked the short one.

"Wish me luck," she said with a sigh.

Jackie and Shea Rodowsky were incredibly enthusiastic. They asked Claudia to draw an advertisement for the sale, which they copied and plastered all over their school. And they managed to convince tons of kids to make donations. Whenever Claudia wasn't sitting, she'd help Jackie and Shea pick up all kinds of things from their friends. Lamps, old chairs, paintings, boxes of books, appliances, silverware — you name it, they lugged it to the Rodowskys'.

It was the same week that Mal, Jessi, and

the Pike kids put together their carnival. It was the same week that the entire *school* seemed to get caught up in a frenzy of giving. I know, because I shared "barn duty" every evening with Mary Anne. Kids were constantly coming over, bringing all kinds of donated clothes and food.

We were impressed with everyone's concern for their pen pals — until some of the kids started asking us for *receipts!* They wanted to make sure they got credit for their donations. When I asked one of them why, he said, "So I can win first prize at the sleepover!" I had to assure them that we were keeping close track of who brought in what.

Claudia noticed how competitive the SES kids were getting, too. Just *how* competitive, she found out that Sunday.

The Rodowskys' yard was every bit as crowded as the Pikes' backyard had been the day before. Claudia and the Rodowskys spent the morning busily piling things onto tables. Even Archie, Jackie's four-year-old brother, helped out.

Jackie and Shea were constantly going into the house and returning with things they hadn't thought of donating, like jewelry and glassware. Ninety-nine percent of the time, Mr. or Mrs. Rodowsky would scold them and make them put the things back.

At one point Jackie ran to Claudia and whispered excitedly. "We got the blender!"

"The blender?" Claudia repeated.

"Yeah," Shea piped up. "Mom and Dad never use it, but Dad didn't want to give it up."

"And I made him feel guilty about not donating to such a good cause," Shea added with a grin.

"They also gave us an old toaster," Jackie said, "and a juice extractor, and a waffle maker, and these glass bowls we've *never* used." He reached over to a table and picked up a heavy glass bowl, wedged in among a lot of appliances. "They're in really great shape, too. Look — "

The edge of the bowl caught on a plastic knob on the toaster. The toaster tipped, nudging a pile of plates. "No!" Claudia shouted.

Too late. The plates fell off and crashed onto the Rodowskys' driveway. Two of them smashed right away.

When the toaster fell, it took care of the others.

"Oh," Jackie said, his mouth hanging open, "sorry."

"Uh, Jackie," Claudia said, stooping to pick up the toaster, "maybe you should get a broom from the garage, okay?"

"Yeah," Jackie said, backing away, "okay."

"Watch it!" Claudia warned, her eyes widening.

Jackie spun around just in time to miss bumping against another table.

With a sigh, Claud picked up the big pieces of the broken plates. (Now you can see why Jackie's nickname is "the walking disaster.") In a moment, Jackie returned unharmed with the broom, and they swept up the rest of the mess. Then Claud went back to setting up the yard. She had to hand it to those boys — they had carefully labeled everything with prices, even sorted things into categories.

By one o'clock (opening time), the yard was set up.

And nobody came — except for Mary Anne and me, but we don't really count. Claudia could feel her heart sink.

But it didn't sink far. By one-twenty the place was hopping. Claudia got so busy she didn't know what hit her.

Well, the sale wasn't even a half-hour old when Mrs. Delaney picked up a big, expensive-looking lamp and said, "Hey, that's *my* lamp!"

Not long afterward, Kristy's stepfather, Watson, strolled over with a big smile. "Hi, Claudia," he said. "What sort of literature are you peddling?"

"Some good stuff!" Claudia said, picking up

the top book from a pile of old, leatherbound books. "Dusti — Doze — " she stammered, reading a spine that said "Dostoevsky." She quickly looked on the front and read the title instead. *"Crime and Punishment!"*

With a smile, Watson picked up the book and began turning pages. "Sorry, but I have this collection. Precious stuff, too. Why would anyone want to — "

Suddenly his face fell. Watson's name was written in faded blue ink on the title page. He put the book down and opened to the title page of another of the books. "Wait a minute . . . this *is* my collection!"

Claudia didn't know what to say. "Oh . . . I can't imagine what . . ."

"David Michael!" Watson called out, his eyes blazing.

David Michael was at the games table, looking at a jigsaw puzzle. He whirled around. "What?" he asked timidly.

"Come here, please," Watson answered.

David Michael slunk over to him with his head down. "What?" he asked again, quietly.

"Did you give the Rodowsky boys these books?"

David Michael's face was turning red. "Well . . . they — they're so *old*, and you never ever read them, and — "

"Watson?" Mrs. Brewer's voice interrupted

her husband. She was walking toward him, holding a box full of dusty picture frames. "Did you know that this was on the table by the porch?"

Watson glared at David Michael.

"They were in the *attic!*" David Michael protested. "And you *said* you wanted to throw them out!"

"It's not only David Michael," Mrs. Brewer said to Watson. "Mrs. Kilbourne found a necklace of hers that Maria had donated, and Mrs. Kuhn — "

Just then, Shea ran by, wailing. His father was following behind, holding a tennis racket and shaking his head angrily. "Seventy-three bucks," he said to Kristy's parents. "If I hadn't seen someone buying it — "

He must have sensed something was up with Kristy's parents, because he stopped. Watson raised an eyebrow and nodded. "We've had a little surprise of our own," he said.

Poor David Michael was almost in tears.

Mr. Rodowsky scrunched up his forehead. "And Mrs. Delaney, and — "

"You better believe that's my radio!" another voice boomed out. "Your father bought it for me for our first anniversary!"

It was Mrs. Addison, scolding her daughter Corrie.

Watson, Mr. Rodowsky, and Mrs. Brewer turned to each other slo-o-owly, their eyes wide and their mouths slightly open. Claudia nearly cracked up.

The next thing they knew, Mr. Rodowsky was standing on a chair, saying, "Attention, everybody! Attention!"

The crowd quieted down. Mr. Rodowsky put on a brave smile and said, "It has come to my attention that certain items at this sale might not be . . . uh, *authorized*. I think some of our collectors have been a little overzealous. I want to offer my apologies, and I hope this won't dampen the spirit of giving. Perhaps we should take a few moments to sort out the sale items from the . . . nonsale items before we go on. And I assure you, if anything is missing, I'll be responsible. Thank you."

There were a few chuckles from the crowd. The first voice Claudia heard was Mrs. Delaney's: "You know, the lamp is a little clunky-looking anyway. I'll let it go."

"Well I *do* want my radio," Mrs. Addison said, then added, "so I'll give you ten dollars for it . . ." She handed a ten-dollar bill to Mrs. Rodowsky, who was behind the table. A smile crept across her face. "After all, it's for the kids, right?"

Most of the parents began chattering with each other and laughing. Watson tapped the book a few times and said, "I'll buy these back for fifteen dollars." He gave a small grin. "Nonnegotiable."

Claudia breathed a sigh of relief. Moments before, she had imagined the whole project falling apart. But it didn't. In fact, it was a big success and raised a lot of money. There were a few more misunderstandings, a few parents dragging their kids home, clutching jewelry or coffeepots. But for the most part, the parents were very understanding. They may have been annoyed, but they acted like . . . well, adults.

Chapter 10

"That's a big box!" I said to Buddy Barrett as he dragged a carton up our driveway.

"Yup," he said. "I can lift it, too."

He did, and his knobby knees shook with the strain.

"Very good, Buddy," I said. "Why don't you put it down and slide it into the barn."

"Okay."

I helped him pull the box in. It was *heavy*. Buddy lives only a couple of houses away, but I was amazed he had struggled to get the box to the barn himself.

"There!" I said, shoving it into a corner. "You know, you're pretty strong for an eight-year-old."

"Yeah," he said, beaming.

"You want me to give you a receipt, Buddy?" I asked, hoping he'd say no.

He nodded eagerly.

For what felt like the hundredth time that day, I grabbed my clipboard from the floor. I had reached the last page of a thick pad of legal paper. The rest of it was covered with inventory, inventory, inventory.

Originally, when I had agreed to let my barn be the storage area for the drives, I thought Mary Anne and I would have an easy job. All we had to do was sit there while kids came and dropped off an occasional box or two. Easy, right?

Wrong.

The carnival and the yard sale had whipped up an unbelievable amount of support for our program. On some days, kids had to stand in line when they brought stuff to the barn.

It was Friday, almost a week after the big weekend, and I felt like I was ready to drop. I lifted out the things in Buddy's box and wrote them down on my pad:

3 prs women's shoes
2 prs women's sneakers
Lt blue sundress
Silk nightgown
Terrycloth robe
4 prs kids' overalls
4 jars tomato sauce
Assorted canned goods
4-lb box, powdered milk
Case powdered baby formula

"Buddy," I said, "are you sure your mom wants to get rid of an entire *case* of formula?"

"Yeah!" Buddy said. "Marnie grew out of that stuff a long time ago."

"And your mom *said* you could take it?"

Buddy rolled his eyes. "*Dawwwwwn*, are you going to give me a receipt or not?"

I was too tired to get into an argument. I quickly scribbled a receipt and Buddy took off. Three more kids came, and I went through the same routine with each. One of them was a kid named Rob Hines. He had been to the barn three times that week.

At a quarter to nine, people stopped coming (finally!). I was sitting on a box, gazing around, when I realized I had spent all this time collecting this stuff but had never really *looked* at it.

And there was a *lot* to look at. About half of the stuff had come in on Mary Anne's days, so I really was seeing it for the first time.

A lot of it was pretty junky, to be honest — stuff I would be embarrassed to send to New Mexico. There were fashions that were prehistoric, like a polyester pale blue leisure suit with stretched-out pockets. There were shoes that were so old and worn, you could tell exactly what the people's feet looked like and how they walked.

But there were also some pretty nice clothes,

and some things that were quite beautiful. I ran my fingers down a gorgeous, silky nightgown with what looked like a hand-painted flower pattern. There were some designer dresses I would die to wear. Someone had brought his-and-her running shoes that looked like they hadn't been worn.

I began snooping around the food section, too. There were mostly cans of tuna, soup, beef stew, and boxes of cereal and flour and raisins. Sensible things — nutritious, inexpensive, and long-lasting. But mixed in with them were six-packs of gum and candy bars, tins of cookies, a box of imported chocolates, a huge canister of cocoa, three jars of caviar . . .

Caviar?

What was that doing here? Who in her right mind would send caviar to people who needed necessities? For that matter, why would anyone send hot cocoa to people who lived in the desert? And the imported chocolates were wonderful, but not exactly necessary.

It seemed funny to me that most parents would donate practical food and clothing while others would give things so off-the-wall.

Unless the parents didn't donate them.

Suddenly the nice stuff didn't seem so . . . *nice*. My eyes traveled to a gray flannel man's suit, hanging near the window. I went to it and opened the lapel.

A tailor's receipt was sticking out of the inner pocket. I pulled it out and read the words scrawled on it.

Under the name HINES was last Wednesday's date.

Mr. Hines had bought a suit last week, had it tailored, and then turned around and given it away?

Something was very wrong. And after what had happened at the yard sale, I had a feeling I knew exactly what.

The next morning, Saturday, I explained my suspicions to Mary Anne over breakfast.

"You know," she said, "I was starting to think something funny was happening, too."

"Why didn't you say anything?" I asked.

"I didn't want to *assume*. Besides, I imagined how happy the pen pals would be when they saw such nice things . . ." She shrugged and sighed. "I guess it was just wishful thinking."

I nodded. "Well, we still don't know for sure, right?"

"Right. Innocent until proven guilty."

"So what should we do?"

Mary Anne took a bite of her grapefruit and thought about it for a moment. "I think we should talk to some of the kids."

"You mean, go to their houses? We can't do that."

"We won't have to, Dawn. The ones who are doing it are probably the ones who keep coming back. They're going for the prizes." She smiled. "We'll just wait for them."

As if on cue, the Hines family drove up. We were *really* in luck. Not only were we going to see Rob, but his parents, too. We met them at their car and walked with them to the barn.

Poor Rob. The minute Mary Anne said, "Thank you for your incredible generosity, Mr. and Mrs. Hines," I could see him start to squirm.

Mr. Hines chuckled. "Oh, no problem. It's nice to know everything will be put to good use."

"Donating the suit was especially nice," Mary Anne continued, gesturing to the gray flannel suit.

I watched the color drain out of Mr. Hines's face (not to mention Rob's). "Why — I — what's that doing here?" he sputtered.

Rob looked back at the car, as if he could make a getaway.

"Rob," Mrs. Hines said.

"Um . . . I . . . I guess I just took it by mistake . . ." Rob said.

Mr. Hines was now rummaging through a box under the suit. "And my wing-tip shoes! I was looking for them yesterday!"

"But you never wear them," Rob said weakly.

"That's not the point," Mrs. Hines replied. "The clothes don't belong to you."

Rob hung his head. "I'm sorry."

Mr. Hines sighed. "I'm awfully sorry, girls. I guess this'll have to be an exchange. I'll take back my good clothes and leave you with a couple of bags." There was an embarrassed smile on his face. "I'm afraid what we're leaving won't be quite as nice."

"Anything's welcome," I said.

After the Hinses left we had a few more confrontations. Fortunately, not too many kids had pulled the same trick.

But leave it to Mary Anne to figure out a solution to the problem.

Permission slips!

Now, instead of just taking an inventory and writing out receipts, we also had to check each kid's slip, which was made up by Mary Anne and looked like this:

I (we) ________ hereby acknowledge that as parent(s) / guardian(s) of ________, I have agreed to donate the following items to be sent to the SES sister school in Zuni, New Mexico:

____

____

____

____

____

____

(The lines at the bottom were for a list of donated items and a signature.)

Mary Anne wrote out the first slip, and Richard took her to a shop in town to make copies. From then on, we didn't let any kid drop off boxes without a slip (if they didn't have one, we'd send them home, box and all).

It worked. The kids weren't so . . . *ambitious* after that. And to be honest with you, there were moments when I wished we hadn't been, either.

The drives and the fund-raising were fun, but I was totally exhausted.

Thursday

Yesterday I sat for Matt and Haley Braddock while their parents were at a church committee meeting. I was sort of hoping to take a break from the pen-pal project. I didn't expect to be part of a last-minute fund-raiser.

I also didn't expect to be spending time with Madame Leveaux, Queen of the Gypsies.

"Don't you think it's a great idea, Mary Anne?" Haley said. "I know I can raise money. Please let me be Madame Leveaux. All I have to do is go out front and tell fortunes. Please please please please please?"

"It *is* a great idea," Mary Anne said, "but it's so elaborate. By the time you get ready, I'll have to leave."

"I'm just going to use my Halloween costume!" Haley insisted. "All the stuff is in my room. And I know exactly what to say. I've been practicing!"

"You have? Whose fortunes have you told?"

"I mailed one to my pen pal."

"From Madame Leveaux?"

"Please, Mary Anne," Haley said, ignoring the question. "It's two whole days to the sleepover. I could make so much money . . . you know, for the pen pals."

"Mm-hm," Mary Anne said. She could sense that Haley had her sights set on a prize, and this was a last-ditch effort. On the other hand, Haley *had* been working hard on the project, and she was so determined . . .

"Well, okay," Mary Anne said. "But promise me you'll be happy — whether you make a lot of money or not."

"Yea!" Haley shouted, clapping her hands

and jumping up and down. "Oh, I knew you'd be nice, Mary Anne!"

Haley turned to her brother, Matt, who had just come into the room. Matt was looking at her expectantly, waiting for her to tell him what was going on.

Matt was born deaf. He's attended a special school for the hearing impaired in Stamford since he was two. Haley talks to him by using Ameslan, or American Sign Language. It's beautiful to watch — all these quick, delicate finger movements — but it's very hard to learn. Of all us baby-sitters, only Jessi has learned to use it well.

Haley signed to Matt with an excited expression on her face. Matt smiled and immediately ran down to the basement. Haley disappeared into her bedroom.

For about two minutes, Mary Anne had some peace.

Then Haley emerged, dressed in an outrageous gypsy costume, something like the genie's outfit in *I Dream of Jeannie*. A fringed, sheer, black veil covered her face.

"Greetings!" she said, rolling the *r*. She began doing her idea of an exotic dance — wiggling awkwardly with her hands over her head, palms together.

Mary Anne burst out laughing.

Haley stopped and said, "Vhat? You dare to laugh at zee famous Ma*dahm* Leveaux?"

"Who are you supposed to sound like?" Mary Anne asked.

"Thees eez zuh vay vee speek een Trannnsylvania," Haley replied.

"Transylvania? Leveaux is a *French* name!"

"I moved vhen I vas a very leetle girl."

"Oh, *that* explains it," Mary Anne said.

"What do you think?" Haley said in her normal voice. "Pretty good, huh?"

"Definitely . . . one of a kind," Mary Anne replied. "Now let's hurry. Your parents come back in about an hour."

There was a sudden clatter from the basement stairs. Matt burst through the door to the kitchen, holding a card table under one arm. He gave it to Haley, then signed something to her and ran back downstairs.

"He's going to get two chairs," Haley explained. "All we need now is a sign."

"I'll make it," Mary Anne said.

Haley ran into the study and brought Mary Anne a piece of paper and some Magic Markers. Mary Anne drew a big sign that looked like this:

By that time, Matt was back from the basement with two folding chairs. He nodded and smiled when he read the sign.

"Perfect!" Haley squealed. "Ooh, this is going to be so great — I mean, zees veel be a vonderful opportunity for zee great Ma*dahm* Leveaux."

"Come, Ma*dahm*," Mary Anne said, imitating her accent. She led the two Braddock kids out the front door. Mary Anne held the table and a chair, Matt held another chair, and Haley held the sign (plus a pack of playing cards she'd found in her room).

Mary Anne set up the table by the sidewalk. Then Haley began spreading the playing cards on top in neat piles, as if she knew what she was doing. Matt signed something to Haley and ran back inside.

She shook her head, annoyed.

"What did he say?" Mary Anne asked.

"He promises to help," Haley replied, "but he wants to practice catching fly balls while we're waiting for customers."

Matt emerged again, wearing a New York Mets cap and a baseball mitt. He quietly threw the ball high in the air and caught it, sometimes sprawling on the ground for dramatic effect.

Before long, Haley had a customer.

Mrs. Barrett, Buddy's mom, came walking by with her two girls, Suzi and Marnie. The minute she saw Haley, she flashed a dazzling smile.

"Well, well," she said, "who do we have here?"

"I am zee great Ma*dahm* Leveaux!" Haley announced. "As eet says on zee sign!"

"So it does!" Mrs. Barrett said. "It is a great honor to meet you, Madame."

Suzi tried to curtsy, but Marnie just stood there, staring blankly at Haley and clutching her mom's hand. (Suzi's five but Marnie's only two.)

"Zee honor eez mine," Haley said. She gestured grandly to the empty folding chair, which Matt pulled backward as if he were a waiter in a fancy restaurant. "Please, one of you have a seat and I vill look into your future! Suzi? Marrrnie?"

"Can I, Mommy?" Suzi said excitedly.

"Sure," Mrs. Barrett said, letting go of Marnie and reaching into her purse for a quarter. "And then it's your sister's turn."

Marnie grabbed her mom's skirt. She didn't look excited at all.

As soon as Suzi sat down, Haley placed her right hand on Suzi's forehead. "Shavoom, shaloom . . ." she chanted. "Mmm-hm. Ah-hah!" With her left hand, she began shuffling the playing cards around. "Very eenteresting!"

"What? *What?*" Suzi pleaded.

"You have a brother, no?" Haley asked.

"Yeah, Buddy," Suzi said. "You know him, Haley!"

"Haley? Who eez Haley? I am zee great Ma*dahm* Leveaux!"

"Oh. Sorry."

"Yes. Vell, I see your brother in a very beeg room, with . . . large hoops and nets in it."

"A gym!" Suzi said.

"Jeem . . . yes, jeem!" Haley replied. She shuffled the cards some more. "I see some sort of . . . party, and many children wearing pajamas and eating pizza . . ."

"The sleepover!" Suzi said.

"Ah, yes, zat must be it," Haley took her hand away from Suzi's head and sat back. "You see, Ma*dahm* Leveaux has correctly predicted zee future! Next, please."

"Hey, no fair, Haley!" Suzi said. "You knew about it already!"

"Honey . . ." Mrs. Barrett said soothingly.

"I want our money back!" Suzi cried out, standing up.

"Suzi, it's all right. Let Marnie have her fortune told, and maybe we can come back later for another try. Buddy's waiting for us." She pulled Marnie toward Haley.

"Ah, Ma*dahm* Leveaux *loves* zee leetle ones!" Haley said.

The feeling was definitely not mutual. "No!" Marnie shrieked. Her face turned bright red and she burst into hysterical crying.

Mrs. Barrett sighed and lifted Marnie to her shoulder. "That's okay, baby," she said. Then to Mary Anne and Haley, "Sorry, girls. I guess we'd better go."

The Barretts left. Matt, who had been looking concerned about Marnie, shrugged and went back to catching fly balls.

"I guess the veil scared her," Haley said.

"These things happen," Mary Anne replied. "And by the way, Haley, it's okay to make things up. You don't have to be accurate."

"Okay," Haley said.

Things went well for the next hour or so. Haley was great. As more people came, she grew more confident. Mary Anne said she was such a ham that it was hard not to laugh. The kids loved her and their parents seemed to get a kick out of her, too.

Then Mary Anne spotted Alan Gray, Justin Forbes, and Pete Black walking across the street. She rolled her eyes and hoped they'd stay there.

Why? Well, first of all, Alan Gray is about the most immature guy in the eighth grade. He once spent hours at a party putting yellow M&M's in his eyes and saying he was Little Orphan Annie. He also has a crush on Kristy, which drives her absolutely *crazy*. Justin's claim to fame with the Baby-sitters is that he once made a prank call to Stacey, saying he was from the Atlanta Pig Farm. Pete actually isn't so bad, but when he's around Alan the immaturity sometimes rubs off.

Mary Anne was sure that if they came over to see "Madame Leveaux," the boys would *really* act dumb, and she'd never be able to get rid of them. So she hoped they wouldn't see Haley. Anyway, they were walking fast, laughing about something. "Let's call them over," Haley said.

"Uh, let's not," Mary Anne replied.

"Why not?"

But it was too late. Alan saw them and said, "Hey, look!"

Sure enough, the boys ran across the street. Alan read Haley's sign, pronouncing her name, "Madam Levy-oox."

"It's Luh-VOH," Haley said. "And vhat may I do for you boys?"

They laughed when they heard her accent. "I want my fortune told!" Alan said, plopping down in the folding chair. "Okay, Madamee Lee-voke-see-odor?"

See what I mean about Alan? He's such a goon. And of course, the other two thought he was unbelievably funny.

"All fortunes are a quarter, please," Haley said, not letting herself be intimidated.

"What?" Alan said. "You wouldn't do mine for free?"

"I have a quarter," Pete said, pulling one out of his pocket and putting it on the table.

Haley shuffled her cards around, chanting, "Sha-voom, sha-loom . . ."

Alan looked up at his two friends and exploded with giggles.

"For you, zee great Ma*dahm* sees — " She stopped herself and gasped. "Oh, I do not believe thees!"

"What?" Alan said, just calming down from his giggling spell.

"I haf never seen cards like thees in my career!"

"Oh, yeah?" Alan was looking at the cards now, interested. "What do you see?"

"I see you as a young man — very handsome, too — " Haley began.

"Alaaan," Justin said with a sly smile.

"Quiet," Alan snapped.

Haley moved her cards around some more. Her voice rose with excitement. "I see riches, lots of success, and great fame. Oh, my goodness! You vill be known throughout zee world as a famous — " She stopped suddenly.

"Famous what?" Alan demanded. "Famous what?"

"I haf given you zee twenty-fife-cent fortune," Haley said solemnly. "For more, you must pay another quarter."

"Oh." Alan quickly took a quarter out of his pocket. "Here, go on."

"Hey!" Pete said. "You *did* have one — "

"I'll pay you back," Alan told him quickly. "Go ahead," he said to Haley.

Haley laid it on thick, telling Alan he was going to be a movie star or something. Of course, the boys pretended they weren't taking it seriously, but all three of them insisted on having their fortunes told. Haley ended up collecting two whole dollars from them. She just made up stuff they wanted to hear, and they were happy to pay for more.

She said she felt guilty afterward, but Mary Anne told her not to worry about it.

To be honest, I couldn't help but feel kind of proud of her.

Where was *I* Wednesday? Frantically making last-minute phone calls about the sleepover. It was in *two days!* And there was still so much to do. Where had the time gone? (Well, most of it had been spent in the barn.)

I couldn't wait for Mary Anne to get back from the Braddocks'. I knew her calm, organized mind would ease my nerves. I must have looked at my watch a hundred times.

Finally, she arrived. Mary Anne quickly told me about Madame Leveaux, and then we got started.

"Okay," she said. "Did you talk to the guy at the *Stoneybrook News*?"

"Uh-huh," I said. "He actually interviewed

me over the phone! He's going to come once at the beginning and once at the end — both times with a photographer."

"Great. How about the pizza place?"

"Yup. They're donating as many pies as we need — and they want to bring them when the photographer is there."

"The toy store?"

"Same thing. They'll donate the prizes, but they wanted to know when the photographer was coming."

"I guess it's good publicity," Mary Anne said.

"Well, they deserve it," I replied.

"Mm-hm. And the teachers are all coming?"

"Four of them. They're bringing their own sleeping bags. There're also going to be three cafeteria workers in the morning, who are volunteering to cook breakfast — and the supermarket is donating pancake mix and juice!"

"Great work, Dawn!" Mary Anne said. "I guess you didn't have time to start working on the schedule . . ."

"I've thought about it," I said. "And I think we should organize a clean-up time at night and in the morning, but I don't think we should do too much else."

"No?"

"Don't you think it would be more fun to

just let the kids have a good time, without *making* them do things?"

"Yeah, but what if they get bored, or what if they go wild? We should have a plan to fall back on — and if we don't have to use it, great!"

For the next hour or so, we worked on a schedule of games and activities. But even after we finished, we couldn't stop talking about it. I don't know *what* time it was when Mary Anne slumped out of my room and went to bed.

The countdown was beginning. I was so excited, I couldn't imagine making it through one more day.

"How do you hook the tape deck to the speakers?"

"Can you bring the ladder over here?"

"Where's Claudia?"

"Yeouch!"

"You *can't* cancel!"

"Hi, Ms. Besser!"

"Over here!"

"Move it to the right!"

Friday was here! (Could you guess?)

It was almost six o'clock, the official starting time of the sleepover. There was so much shouting and running around in the gym, I don't know how we got anything done (and that was *before* any kids arrived!)

By the way, my voice was the one saying, "You *can't* cancel!" I was on the pay phone just outside the gym. Mr. Morton, the owner of the Pizza Express, was telling me his special shipment of flour hadn't arrived. I was so upset, I could barely speak. "What are the kids going to eat?" I said, almost in tears.

"I'm sorry," Mr. Morton said. "I understand your problem, but I can't make pizza without flour. And I'm paying two men to hang around and do nothing, so — "

"Isn't there another place where you can get flour?"

"Not this late — and not for thirty pies."

"But the kids'll think you let them down, Mr. Morton," I said. "They've grown up with your pizza, and they love it so much."

"*I'm* not letting them down," Mr. Morton said. "It's . . . circumstances."

I sighed. "I guess that's just what I'll have to tell them," I said. "Maybe someday they'll understand. Um, there's a pizza place in Mercer that stays open late, isn't there? Do you happen to have their number?"

Mr. Morton was silent for a moment or two. Then he said, "You know, maybe I can call Jerry at the IGA supermarket. Would you mind if some of the pies were whole wheat?"

"Not at all!" I practically shouted. "Oh, Mr. Morton, you're the greatest!"

I hung up and ran into the gym. Just inside the door, Mary Anne was fiddling with wires at the back of a tape deck while two teachers watched. Mal and Jessi were helping Ms. Besser spread wrestling mats on the floor. Kristy was organizing the table setup for the pizzas and prizes. Stacey and Claudia were putting up decorations — streamers, posters of New Mexico, pictures and souvenirs sent by the Zuni pen pals.

It felt like seven years had passed since Wednesday night. We spent part of Thursday at SES, arranging final details. (That's when we found out that almost a hundred kids had signed up!) That night Mary Anne and I counted the money that had been collected (more about that later). Then, on Friday afternoon, everything went wrong at once. First the reporter didn't think he'd make it because he was covering some town meeting that ran late. Then Ms. Reynolds wasn't able to get the CD player she had promised, so Mary Anne had to convince Richard to let her bring her tape deck. Then there was the problem with the pizza . . .

Well, I won't bore you with all the details. The point is, now things were *finally* coming together.

Just after six, Watson dropped off David Michael Thomas. I was *so* happy — the sleepover had finally begun!

For the next hour or so, kids poured in, all of them carrying overnight bags. Haley was one of the first, and so were Buddy Barrett and Becca Ramsey. Soon there was a traffic jam of parents and kids by the gym door. Dozens of voices blended together:

" 'Bye, sweetheart!" . . . "Don't forget to brush your teeth!" . . . "Get some sleep, or you'll be tired tomorrow." . . . "Where's the pizza?" . . . "I don't want to sleep on those yucky mats!" . . . "What if I have to 'go' in the middle of the night?" . . .

I'll let you guess which were the parents and which were the kids.

Finally, Mr. Selden, one of the teachers, had to announce, "Would everyone please move into either the gym or the hallway? We need to keep the entrance clear!"

In a far corner, I noticed some kids rolling out sleeping bags. "Hey, guys!" I called. "Don't worry about that yet, okay? There's going to be a lot of running around before bedtime!"

"WHO BUILT THE ARK? NOAH! NOAH!"

Suddenly the voice of Raffi blared out of the speakers so loudly that I had to cover my ears. Immediately the volume went down and a timid voice said, "It works!" Mary Anne had finally gotten the tape player hooked up.

"No kidding," Shea Rodowsky remarked, followed by a burst of giggles.

At a quarter to seven, the reporter and photographer showed up. I introduced myself, then let them roam around the room.

The kids thought this was just about the coolest thing in the world. The reporter conducted interviews with a cassette recorder while the photographer flashed away. I overheard one boy say into the mike, "I intend to pursue my ambition to become a neuro — neurolog — neurobiolo — can I start over?"

It was around then that I noticed a little boy whose lip was starting to quiver. "Are you all right?" I asked him, kneeling down.

He frowned and nodded his head, but the moment I turned around, he couldn't hold it in any longer. *"I want my mommy to take me home!"* he cried.

"Oh, it'll be okay," I said as reassuringly as I could.

"Ahh wahhh mahhh mahhhmahhh . . . right nowww!" he said (that's roughly what he said — it was hard to understand him).

One thing about crying, it's contagious. Two or three other kids began to sob softly. Mary Anne went to one, Claudia to another. Then there was an outbreak of tears on the other side of the gym. For a moment I panicked. Were we going to have to send all the kids home — after their hard work? Who was going to eat the pizza?

Fortunately, we only had to call two kids'

parents. Those kids left happily, and the rest of them recovered — especially when 7:05 rolled around.

Why 7:05? Because that's when the pizzas came! You could tell they were here the minute the truck pulled into the parking lot. The smell was *incredible*.

And so was the noise. Kids pushed each other to get to the pies even before the delivery men set them down.

"Hold it!" Ms. Besser called out. "Everyone sit down. The pizzas will not be opened until everyone is sitting!"

Reluctantly, the kids obeyed. They watched, practically drooling, as the delivery men brought in boxes of pizza, crates of soda, and stacks of paper plates and napkins. Mr. Morton supervised them (and managed to get himself into a few photos).

Ms. Besser picked several of the older kids to help us baby-sitters distribute slices around the room. It was a big job, and if I had a dime for each time someone said "I'm finished!" I'd have been rich.

Needless to say, the pizzas disappeared within minutes (except for a few slices with anchovies). They were good, too — especially the ones made with whole-wheat flour.

But let me tell you, *no* pizza is good when it's cold and lying on an abandoned, grease-covered plate. And there were plenty of those left — many of them from the kids who shouted, "I'm finished." (Thank you very much.)

And guess which seven girls had to clean up?

Actually, we didn't mind much, because it meant that the worst part was over. The toy store people were due to come any minute with the delivery of prizes. Then the fun could really begin.

The reporter and photographer were long gone by the time the toy store people came. The toy store people didn't seem to mind, though.

They sure were popular with the kids. It was as if Santa had arrived in the room. You could feel a shiver of excitement going through the gym.

As the delivery people left, we did a quick inventory of the prizes and figured out which ones would go to which kids. Then Ms. Besser called out in her best teacher-voice, "Listen up, everybody. This is what you've been waiting for!"

"Oooh, awards! Awards!" Haley yelled.

The kids stampeded toward us.

As Kristy, Stacey, Ms. Besser, and a couple of other teachers helped the kids to spread out, I turned to Mary Anne. I had just realized the one thing we hadn't talked about. "Mary

Anne, who's going to give out the prizes?"

"You are," Mary Anne answered matter-of-factly.

"Me?"

"Why not? You've done more work than any of us. Why shouldn't you be the one the kids go crazy over?"

"Yeah, but what am I going to say?" I asked.

"You'll think of something," Mary Anne said. "Just like that day in the auditorium."

"Yes, but — "

"Go ahead. Everyone's expecting you to do it."

By now the kids were silent — and staring right at me. So were Kristy, Stacey, Mal, Claudia, and Jessi.

I cleared my throat and picked up my master tally sheet, which I had spent all Thursday night working on.

"Uh, welcome to the Awards Ceremony!" I said.

The kids cheered and clapped. It was as if they were on a TV game show.

I decided to play right into it. "Behind me are the prizes you've been waiting for, courtesy of your favorite store, the Toy Chest!"

More cheers.

"Are you ready, Mary Anne Spier?" I asked.

"Ready!" Mary Anne said, her hands poised over the boxes of gifts.

"Are you ready?" I asked the kids.

"Ready!" came the incredibly loud answer.

"I can't quite hear you!"

"READY!"

"Okay, may I have a drumroll, please . . ."

Kristy started drumming her hands on the table. A few kids in the front joined in — and before long, the floor was vibrating.

I finally had to yell, "Okay, stop!"

It didn't work, so I decided to go on, in a soft voice. "The winner for . . ."

Instantly the room was silent. "The winner for most creative fund-raising idea . . . Haley Braddock!"

"Yea!" Haley yelled as she sprang up.

"Let's have a hand for Haley, our own Madame Leveaux!"

The kids cheered, and Mary Anne handed me Haley's gift. "For your continued study of the stars, this fine telescope!"

"Really?" Haley said. She ripped open the box, pulled out a brand-new miniature telescope, and held it in the air. "Oh, thanks, Dawn!"

As she ran back to her seat, I announced, "And now for the person who donated the most clothes . . ."

This time I didn't have to ask for the drumroll.

". . . Rob Hines!"

The ceremony went on like this. There were a dozen main prizes, all of them really nice — a skateboard, roller skates, video games, a sled, among others. We tried to spread the gifts to as many kids as possible. For instance, the Pikes shared a croquet set.

I was afraid some of the kids would feel sad or bitter about not winning. But the toy store people had thought of that in advance. They had included a big bag of tiny prizes — buttons, stickers, coloring books, and puzzles. Everyone ended up getting some kind of reward.

When the awards were over, I thanked everybody and gave a little speech about helping the pen pals. Then, putting aside my clipboard, I announced, "Okay, it's game time! What do you want to play?"

"Red Rover!" someone shouted.

"Spud!"

"Red Light, Green Light!"

"Mother, May I?"

"All right, if you want to play Red Light, Green Light, come to me," I said.

"I'll take the Spud people!" Kristy volunteered.

"Mary Anne and I will do Red Rover!" Stacey said.

"Mal and I will do Mother, May I?" Jessi piped up.

For about an hour, the kids went wild. Then we switched them over to quieter games — I Spy, Telephone, Ghost, Grandmother's Trunk. It was almost nine o'clock.

The children began to wind down. The teachers had thought to bring a huge selection of books for all different age levels. Before long, the gym was divided into small circles of kids. Each circle was being read to by a teacher or a BSC member. I read *One Morning in Maine* by Robert McCloskey, mostly to seven-year-olds. By the time I got to the last line, "Clam chowder for lunch!", I could see a few heavy eyelids.

It was the perfect time to give them the best news of the night. I excused myself and got up. Then I went to my clipboard and announced, "Uh, before you all go to bed — "

There were a few groans, but not many.

" — I think you might like to know the grand total of the money you raised for your pen pals." I made a big deal of flipping through the legal pad, then read the figure.

It was a phenomenal total. I couldn't believe it myself when we had added it up. I had made Stacey count it about four times.

There were some gasps and wow's, then a few kids began to applaud.

I was proud of the kids, and glad they realized how impressive the total was. I began clapping, too. "Go ahead," I said. "Give yourselves a hand. You deserve it!"

They did, and you know what? The looks of satisfaction on their faces were almost enough to make me forget about all the days of hard work.

Almost.

It was bedtime, and trying to put a hundred tired elementary-school kids to sleep is no small task. We started with the second-graders, and took them to the boys' and girls' rooms, where they could change in the privacy of the stalls. Some of them were so tired we practically had to carry them. Then we waited patiently while they washed up and brushed their teeth — or refused to wash and brush. *Then* we went back for the next bunch.

A little before ten, something happened that I don't think I'll forget for a long time. There was a little boy who had been very quiet that night, a second-grader whose name I didn't know. I remembered that he'd brought a few things to the garage that first week — not a huge amount, but a couple of good-size boxes. I also remembered that he never looked at me in the barn. He seemed embarrassed.

He was very tired after washing up, but as I walked with him to his sleeping bag, he looked straight into my eyes. "Is Johnny going to have dinners, too, now?"

"Johnny?" I asked.

"My pen pal," the boy said. "He told me he wasn't having dinners 'cause his house burned up, and he has to stay in a hotel."

"I . . . I hope so," I said.

"I donated lots of dinner food — tuna, and soup, and stuff like that."

"Well, then, the answer is yes," I said, as I helped him unzip his sleeping bag. "We'll make sure Johnny has dinners."

The boy crawled into the bag. As he snuggled into a comfortable position, there was a happy smile on his face. He looked at me again and said, "Thanks, Dawn. You're the nicest girl I ever met."

"I . . . I . . . I . . . I . . ."

The voice was coming out in frightened little hiccups. I didn't know the girl, but for some reason she had decided to come to me.

It was 10:09, and I was almost done tucking in the children. "What is it?" I asked, taking the girl's hand. "Don't worry, I'm listening."

"I . . . I . . . I don't want to stay here!"

"Aren't you having a good time?" I asked. She must have been. She'd been running around like crazy all night.

"Uh-huh," she said, nodding her head.

"Did someone hit you?"

"Uh-uh." She shook her head no.

"Then what's wrong?"

She shrugged. "I just want to go home."

"Oh," I said. "You feeling a little lonely?"

She nodded.

"You feel funny not sleeping in your own bed?"

She nodded harder.

"Okay, come with me." I took the girl into the hallway and called her parents. They were very understanding and came right away.

When they left, it was 10:21. All of the kids were in their sleeping bags by then. Not that they were *asleep*, of course. Many of them got their second wind as soon as they were down. There were little pockets of giggling conversation all over the room. Every once in awhile, someone would say "Sssshhh!" and the talking would stop — for a few seconds.

This went on until eleven or so. By that time, most of the kids were asleep or almost asleep.

Me? I was ready to drop, too. I was standing (barely) with the teachers and the rest of the BSC members under one of the basketball hoops.

It was the first chance I had had to talk to Ms. Besser all night. "Congratulations, Dawn," she said, smiling broadly. "I've never seen anything quite like this come off so well. I only wish your brother could have been here to see it. He would have been proud."

I nodded. I wished Jeff had been there, too. It was hard not to miss him at a time like this.

Ms. Besser turned to all of the BSC members. "You all deserve nothing but the highest praise."

I was tired, but not too tired to smile.

"Thanks," I said. "But if it weren't for you, this would never have happened."

Everyone agreed with me. Ms. Besser returned my smile and said, "Do me a favor. Would you mind staying exactly the same age for a few years until I have a child old enough to be baby-sat for?"

We laughed. Some of the kids turned in their sleeping bags to see what was going on.

"We'll see what we can do," I said. I paused. "I don't know about anyone else, but I'm *tired*.

"Me, too," said Mary Anne, Claudia, and a couple of the teachers.

It was our turn to use the rest rooms, which was fun, like summer camp, but we kept quiet to avoid disturbing the kids.

Sometime around 11:20 I fell asleep.

At 11:31 I heard a girl say, "I have to go to the *bath*room!"

"Go ahead," Mary Anne's sleepy voice replied.

"I can't," the girl said.

"Why not?"

"I'm afraid!"

When I heard footsteps, I dozed again.

But not for long. "*I* have to go to the bathroom!" someone else announced.

"Me, too!"

"Me, too!"

The second voice came from nearby. Wearily

I rounded up three kids. Wearily I marched them to the rest rooms. Wearily I walked them back.

I tried to go to sleep again — several times. Just when I would be starting a wonderful dream, some crisis would occur.

At 11:52, Jordan Pike got into a fight over where he and another boy had the right to put their feet while they slept.

At 12:06, a girl had a screaming nightmare. That was not fun. While Stacey calmed her down, two other kids began to cry and had to be comforted.

I don't know *when* these things happened:

Buddy Barrett started sleepwalking, and Mr. Selden followed him patiently all around the gym without waking him up. (For some reason, you're not supposed to wake up a sleepwalker.)

A fifth-grader got a charlie horse.

A second-grader had an . . . *accident* in a sleeping bag and woke up crying.

Someone had eaten too much pizza. (Fortunately, a teacher got him to the bathroom in time!)

Throughout the night, there were clusters of kids wanting to be taken to the bathroom — one would speak up, and the rest would follow.

* * *

Needless to say, when morning came, none of us had slept much.

The supermarket delivery people came around 5:30, and we let them into the cafeteria, which was down the hall.

About twenty minutes later, the cafeteria volunteers arrived. They went quietly to work.

I think I will never forget the smell of pancakes that started seeping into the gym. I'm not a big fan of pancakes, but smelling them that morning made me weak with hunger.

It also started rousing the kids. You'd think they had had the deepest, most peaceful night's sleep in their lives.

It was a new day, and they were raring to go, to say the least.

"I'm hungry!" one kid called out.

"Where's the TV?" another demanded.

Another started laughing, exclaiming, "Look at Jimmy's *hair!*"

The boy named Jimmy, whose curly hair had gone wild in the night, furiously tried to press it down.

A group of boys ran around with their sleeping bags tied around their necks like capes, shooting imaginary space-age weapons.

Somehow, us older people managed to arrange them into groups for wash-up time. Then, of course, they had to dress themselves in the stalls, which was another adventure.

Some of them took *forever*. Some didn't want to be seen in clothes that had gotten so wrinkled overnight. Others teased their friends for no good reason.

I thought the pancakes would turn to rocks by the time we got everyone to the cafeteria.

They didn't. In fact, they were incredible — *much* better than the meals I had in my elementary school. The kids had a choice of plain, blueberry, strawberry, or buttermilk pancakes. There was plenty of syrup and butter. And there was orange, apple, and grapefruit juice, and lots of milk and coffee.

"My, you look slightly less than perfect!" Stacey said to me with a teasing smile.

"I feel like I've been run over by a truck," I replied.

Stacey held out a glass of orange juice. "Here, have some of this. It'll wake you up."

I shook my head. "No thanks."

My eyelids felt as if they weighed about a ton. And I really needed to be wide awake, because breakfast was like — well, you can imagine what breakfast for a hundred kids was like.

"Hey!" Vanessa Pike suddenly shouted. A pancake had ended up on her head, and a few kids were covering their mouths and laughing. I took her away to the girls' room.

By the time I got back, every teacher and

baby-sitter had his or her hands full.

"Ew!" cried a group of girls, pulling their trays away from a huge syrup spill on a table.

Splat! Jackie Rodowsky landed on his backside when he slipped on some spilled grapefruit juice.

"Hey, look at me!" Byron Pike was entertaining a group of boys by putting two strips of pancake under his nose to look like a mustache.

"Charlene took my juice!" a girl started shouting.

"Well, you took my seat!" That must have been Charlene.

This went on . . . and on . . . and on . . .

Until Claudia poked me in the ribs. "Dawn, do you see what I see?"

I looked up. A smiling man and woman were peering through the cafeteria door.

"Daddy! Mommy!" a second-grader called out.

"Parents!" I said, like someone stranded in the desert might say "Water!"

As more and more parents came, the chaos started again. Kids returned their trays (or didn't), went back to the gym, lost their stuff, had trouble packing their stuff, mixed their stuff up with someone else's, you name it.

In the midst of all of this, the reporter and photographer came back to do a follow-up report — which delayed things even more.

The Barretts were the last parents to come and the last to leave. As we watched them walk Buddy out to the parking lot, we stood in the door and waved.

Then it was time for *our* celebration.

"Whoopee!" Kristy shouted. "We did it!"

All seven of us baby-sitters somehow managed to embrace each other. The teachers stood around us, smiling.

Then we looked back into the gym.

Strewn around the floor were candy wrappers, shoelaces, toothbrushes, plastic cups, underwear — even a couple of pizza crusts that had been overlooked.

But you know what? Tired as I was, I suddenly felt full of energy. All I could think about was this: My great plan — every last complicated part of it — was over. And boy, had it been a success!

As I cleaned up the remains of the sleepover, I could barely feel my feet touch the ground.

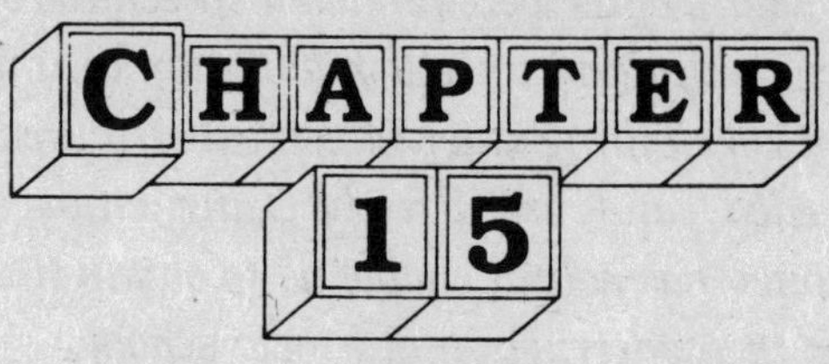

As soon as we had cleaned up, my friends and I gathered at my house with the teachers and bundled everything up to send to Zuni. We loaded cars and Ms. Reynolds's minivan, packing as tightly as we could, and *still* we had to make three trips.

The postal costs came out of the money we collected, but we sent the rest in a check directly to the principal of the Zuni school (super sleuthing on Claudia's part — she found his name in one of the Pike kids' letters, then called New Mexico information for his home address).

A week later, we heard from him. The letter came to SES and went like this:

To the children of Stoneybrook, Connecticut:

I have been an educator for twenty-seven years. As an English teacher and an administrator, I have guided my children to speak clearly with well-chosen words. But for the first time in my life, I find that words are inadequate to express my feelings — our *feelings.*

Many of us were rendered speechless by your generosity and unselfish donation of time. The gifts of clothing and food were distributed where needed, and are already being enjoyed. The money has helped enable us to obtain financing for the construction of a new school.

But the rewards of your work go beyond the gifts themselves. Our children have been inspired by you to do fund-raising of their own. They are planning various activities right now, and the community seems to be throwing its support behind them.

The government, perhaps partly as a reaction to the positive efforts we are displaying, agreed today to grant us substantial disaster funding.

With luck, our school will be built and stocked with supplies by the beginning of next school year.

We hope to be left with a reserve fund for an exchange trip with our brothers and sisters in Stoneybrook, Connecticut.

Once again, thank you all.

Fondly,
Joseph Woodward

Pretty nice, huh? I felt shivers when I read it. Especially the part about "brothers and sisters." I hope there really will be an exchange trip sometime — and I hope a few older kids will be asked to come along to help!

Anyway, in the weeks after the sleepover, there was a lot of pen pal correspondence. Charlotte showed me a great letter from Theresa Bradley.

Dear Char,

Rember in my last letter when I told you my mom was crying alot? Well, when all your stuf came she cryed some more. But now she says its cause shes happy!

I'm happy, to. Is the lether frinjed vest from you? Its realy nice and I got it. I also liked geting a botle of choclit sauce and those cans of pork and beens, even tho my ant had some. I didn't like the deviled ham but that's ok.

My couzin says that now she really wishes her school woud burn down, since she saw what hapened to us.

I still think shes crazy.

Thank you for being so nice to us.

Luv ya,
Theresa
your best number #1 pen pal

And there was a letter that came to Mary Anne's house in an envelope marked like this:

Nancy Green
P.O. Box A7449
Zuni, NM

Madame Leveaux
c/o Mary Anne Spier
177 Burnt Hill Rd.
Stoneybrook, Ct 06800

CAUTION: TO BE OPENED ONLY BY MADAME LEVEAUX

"Um, Haley?" Mary Anne said the night she brought it to the Braddocks'. "Who's Nancy Green?"

"My pen pal," Haley replied. "Why?"

"That's strange," Mary Anne replied, handing her the letter. "Why would she write to you, as Madame Leveaux, at my address?"

"Oh," Haley said, "I — I wrote her a note from Madame Leveaux, you know, as a joke." Haley was starting to squirm. "Well, I didn't want her to know it was from me, so I gave her your address. I meant to tell you, Mary Anne. Really! I just — forgot."

"That doesn't sound like you, Haley," Mary Anne said.

"I know," Haley replied. "I'm not going to do it again. I'm sorry."

"All right," Mary Anne said, turning to go. "See you."

" 'Bye!" Haley quickly closed the door.

As Mary Anne walked home, she couldn't help smiling. What she hadn't told Haley was that she'd opened the letter by mistake and read it already. Haley, as Madame Leveaux, had written her pen pal right around the time of the assembly. That was when I had asked all the kids not to tell their pen pals about our plans. Haley was dying to tell Nancy Green, but she knew she couldn't.

That didn't mean *Madame Leveaux* couldn't tell her . . .

Anyway, this is what the letter said:

Dear Mrs. Leveaux,

You were right. Everything you said, all that stuff about help coming from a mysterious place in the east, it all came true. When I told my friends about your predictions, nobody believed me. Then, the day after your letter came, we got this great stuff from our pen pals. Clothes, food, even a huge check to build a new school! I can't believe my pen pal, Haley Braddock, never mentioned anything about it!

Now here are some questions for you.

Did you know our pen pals are in the same exact town you live in? How did you know my address? How did you know about Pens Across America?

Anyway, thank you for sending the fortune. Please send me another one. My friends and I can't wait!

Yours truly,
Nancy Green

P.S. This time, Haley, disguise your handwriting better!

About the Author

Ann M. Martin did *a lot* of baby-sitting when she was growing up in Princeton, New Jersey. Now her favorite baby-sitting charge is her cat, Mouse, who lives with her in her Manhattan apartment.

Ann Martin's Apple Paperbacks include *Yours Turly, Shirley*; *Ten Kids, No Pets*; *With You and Without You*; *Bummer Summer*; and all the other books in the Baby-sitters Club series.

She is a former editor of books for children, and was graduated from Smith College. She likes ice cream, the beach, and *I Love Lucy*; and she hates to cook.

Look for #45

KRISTY AND THE BABY PARADE

I picked up a recent issue of the *Stoneybrook News,* thinking that I might find some interesting things for David Michael and Emily to cut out. Most of what I glanced at looked fairly boring, though. There was a long story about the new sewage treatment plant, and another about some people's fiftieth wedding anniversary.

I kept leafing through the paper, looking for good pictures. Then this ad caught my eye. "Calling All Babies!" it said. It was an ad for the Stoneybrook Baby Parade.

I remembered some of the baby parades I'd seen. They were pretty crazy! Every entry has to have a "theme" — and some of the themes are kind of . . . well, imaginative. Like the float one year that was called "Circus Days." It had a twelve-foot-high elephant on wheels! Or the "Wild West" float I saw once, with a whole cowboys-and-indians pageant being acted out on top of it.

Babies in strollers had to have themes, too — they'd be dressed up like fairy-tale characters or people in the movies.

It was pretty silly, all right.

But after I'd read that ad, my glance kept resting on Emily Michelle. She is *ador*able. Did I already tell you that? Well, she is. I looked at her glossy, straight black hair cut like a Dutch girl's. I looked at her sparkling brown almond-shaped eyes. I looked at her plump, pink cheeks and at her sturdy little hands (all covered with glue at the moment, but still very cute) and at her round little tummy.

I was getting an idea.

Read all the books
in the Baby-sitters Club series
by Ann M. Martin

1 *Kristy's Great Idea*
Kristy's great idea is to start *The Baby-sitters Club*!

2 *Claudia and the Phantom Phone Calls*
Someone mysterious is calling Claudia!

3 *The Truth About Stacey*
Stacey's different . . . and it's harder on her than anyone knows.

4 *Mary Anne Saves the Day*
Mary Anne is tired of being treated like a baby. It's time to take charge!

5 *Dawn and the Impossible Three*
Dawn thought she'd be baby-sitting — not *monster*-sitting!

6 *Kristy's Big Day*
Kristy's a baby-sitter — and a bridesmaid, too!

7 *Claudia and Mean Janine*
Claudia's big sister is super smart . . . and super *mean*.

8 *Boy-Crazy Stacey*
Stacey's too busy being *boy-crazy* to baby-sit!

9 *The Ghost at Dawn's House*
Creaking stairs, a secret passage — there must be a ghost at Dawn's house!

#10 *Logan Likes Mary Anne!*
Mary Anne has a crush on a *boy* baby-sitter!

#11 *Kristy and the Snobs*
The kids in Kristy's new neighborhood are S-N-O-B-S!

#12 *Claudia and the New Girl*
Claudia might give up the club — and it's all Ashley's fault!

#13 *Good-bye Stacey, Good-bye*
Oh, no! Stacey McGill is moving back to New York!

#14 *Hello, Mallory*
Is Mallory Pike good enough to join the club?

#15 *Little Miss Stoneybrook . . . and Dawn*
Everyone in Stoneybrook has gone beauty-pageant crazy!

#16 *Jessi's Secret Language*
Jessi's new charge is teaching her a *secret language*.

#17 *Mary Anne's Bad-Luck Mystery*
Will Mary Anne's bad luck ever go away?

#18 *Stacey's Mistake*
Has Stacey made a big mistake by inviting the Baby-sitters to New York City?

#19 *Claudia and the Bad Joke*
Claudia is headed for trouble when she baby-sits for a practical joker.

#20 *Kristy and the Walking Disaster*
Can Kristy's Krushers beat Bart's Bashers?

#21 *Mallory and the Trouble With Twins*
Sitting for the Arnold twins is double trouble!

#22 *Jessi Ramsey, Pet-sitter*
Jessi has to baby-sit for a house full of . . . *pets!*

#23 *Dawn on the Coast*
Could Dawn be a California girl for good?

#24 *Kristy and the Mother's Day Surprise*
Emily Michelle is the big surprise!

#25 *Mary Anne and the Search for Tigger*
Tigger is missing! Has he been catnapped?

#26 *Claudia and the Sad Good-bye*
Claudia never thought she'd have to say good-bye to her grandmother.

#27 *Jessi and the Superbrat*
Jessi gets to baby-sit for a TV star!

#28 *Welcome Back, Stacey!*
Stacey's moving again . . . back to Stoneybrook!

#29 *Mallory and the Mystery Diary*
Only Mal can solve the mystery in the old diary.

#30 *Mary Anne and the Great Romance*
Mary Anne's father and Dawn's mother are getting *married!*

#31 *Dawn's Wicked Stepsister*
Dawn thought having a stepsister was going to be fun. Was she ever wrong!

#32 *Kristy and the Secret of Susan*
Even Kristy can't learn all of Susan's secrets.

#33 *Claudia and the Great Search*
There are *no* baby pictures of Claudia. Could she have been . . . adopted?!

#34 *Mary Anne and Too Many Boys*
Will a summer romance come between Mary Anne and Logan?

#35 *Stacey and the Mystery of Stoneybrook*
Stacey discovers a *haunted house* in Stoneybrook!

#36 *Jessi's Baby-sitter*
How could Jessi's parents have gotten a *baby-sitter* for her?

#37 *Dawn and the Older Boy*
Will Dawn's heart be broken by an older boy?

#38 *Kristy's Mystery Admirer*
Someone is sending Kristy *love notes!*

#39 *Poor Mallory!*
Mallory's dad has lost his job, but the Pike kids are coming to the rescue!

#40 *Claudia and the Middle School Mystery*
Can the Baby-sitters find out who the cheater is at SMS?

#41 *Mary Anne vs. Logan*
Mary Anne thought she and Logan would be together forever. . . .

#42 *Jessi and the Dance School Phantom*
Someone — or some*thing* — wants Jessi out of the show.

#43 *Stacey's Emergency*
The Baby-sitters are so worried. Something's wrong with Stacey.

#44 *Dawn and the Big Sleepover*
A hundred kids, thirty pizzas — it's Dawn's biggest baby-sitting job ever!

#45 *Kristy and the Baby Parade*
Will the Baby-sitters' float take first prize in the Stoneybrook Baby Parade?

Super Specials:

1 *Baby-sitters on Board!*
Guess who's going on a dream vacation? The Baby-sitters!

2 *Baby-sitters' Summer Vacation*
Good-bye, Stoneybrook . . . hello, Camp Mohawk!

3 *Baby-sitters' Winter Vacation*
The Baby-sitters are off for a week of winter fun!

4 *Baby-sitters' Island Adventure*
Two of the Baby-sitters are shipwrecked!

5 *California Girls!*
A winning lottery ticket sends the Baby-sitters to *California!*

by Ann M. Martin

❑ MG43388-1	#1	Kristy's Great Idea	$3.25
❑ MG43513-2	#2	Claudia and the Phantom Phone Calls	$3.25
❑ MG43511-6	#3	The Truth About Stacey	$3.25
❑ MG43512-4	#4	Mary Anne Saves the Day	$3.25
❑ MG43720-8	#5	Dawn and the Impossible Three	$3.25
❑ MG43899-9	#6	Kristy's Big Day	$3.25
❑ MG43719-4	#7	Claudia and Mean Janine	$3.25
❑ MG43509-4	#8	Boy-Crazy Stacey	$3.25
❑ MG43508-6	#9	The Ghost at Dawn's House	$3.25
❑ MG43387-3	#10	Logan Likes Mary Anne!	$3.25
❑ MG43660-0	#11	Kristy and the Snobs	$3.25
❑ MG43721-6	#12	Claudia and the New Girl	$3.25
❑ MG43386-5	#13	Good-bye Stacey, Good-bye	$3.25
❑ MG43385-7	#14	Hello, Mallory	$3.25
❑ MG43717-8	#15	Little Miss Stoneybrook...and Dawn	$3.25
❑ MG44234-1	#16	Jessi's Secret Language	$3.25
❑ MG43659-7	#17	Mary Anne's Bad-Luck Mystery	$2.95
❑ MG43718-6	#18	Stacey's Mistake	$3.25
❑ MG43510-8	#19	Claudia and the Bad Joke	$3.25
❑ MG43722-4	#20	Kristy and the Walking Disaster	$3.25
❑ MG43507-8	#21	Mallory and the Trouble with Twins	$2.95
❑ MG43658-9	#22	Jessi Ramsey, Pet-sitter	$3.25
❑ MG43900-6	#23	Dawn on the Coast	$3.25
❑ MG43506-X	#24	Kristy and the Mother's Day Surprise	$3.25
❑ MG43347-4	#25	Mary Anne and the Search for Tigger	$3.25
❑ MG42503-X	#26	Claudia and the Sad Good-bye	$3.25
❑ MG42502-1	#27	Jessi and the Superbrat	$2.95
❑ MG42501-3	#28	Welcome Back, Stacey!	$2.95
❑ MG42500-5	#29	Mallory and the Mystery Diary	$3.25
❑ MG42498-X	#30	Mary Anne and the Great Romance	$3.25
❑ MG42497-1	#31	Dawn's Wicked Stepsister	$3.25
❑ MG42496-3	#32	Kristy and the Secret of Susan	$2.95
❑ MG42495-5	#33	Claudia and the Great Search	$2.95
❑ MG42494-7	#34	Mary Anne and Too Many Boys	$2.95

More titles... ➧